THE
INTROSPECTIVE
DETECTIVE

✱ greenhill

Copyright © Michael Downes 2024

All rights reserved. No part of this publication may be reproduced, distributed, or transmitted in any form or by any means, including photocopying, recording, or other electronic or mechanical methods, without the prior written permission of the publisher, except in the case of brief quotations embodied in critical reviews and certain other non-commercial uses permitted by copyright law.

✱ greenhill

https://greenhillpublishing.com.au/

Downes, Michael (author)
The Introspective Detective
ISBN 978-1-923214-87-3
FICTION | CRIME

Typesetting Calluna Regular 11/16
Cover and book design by Green Hill Publishing

THE INTROSPECTIVE DETECTIVE

MICHAEL DOWNES

I wish to acknowledge the assistance given to me by Patricia Cation, Chris Davie, and Gabrielle Downes. Their input into the creative content and structure of this novel has greatly improved the story.

I also want to thank my lovely wife Kimberly, who indulged my writing sessions in our downtime while we were on holiday for several weeks in Europe and later in the USA.

And her parents Dennis and Mary Ellen Weber. For six weeks I often had my head in my laptop while we stayed with them in Indianapolis. My sincere apologies for the lack of conversation during those times.

Thank you.

CHAPTER ONE

Anna was exhausted. It was 12:22 am Thursday morning and the end of an eight-and-a-half-hour shift. She had driven the last scheduled Melbourne Metropolitan train service to the end of the line at Hurstbridge, then stationed the train alongside others in the rail yards. As was her usual routine, she shouldered her bag and began to walk through the six carriages to check that all was in order. If necessary, she would report the need for any extra cleaning to the station supervisor. The train would become active again at 4:55 am.

It was in the second to last carriage that she saw the middle-aged, well-dressed man in a three-piece tweed suit, collared white business shirt and a tie. He was facing her with his head resting on the window, apparently asleep. It didn't often happen but sometimes a tired or intoxicated or drug-affected passenger would fall asleep on the journey home. Such people were almost always casually attired, even untidy, and certainly did not look as sartorially elegant as this man.

His face was completely drained of colour, deathly white except for blueness on his lips. His eyelids were fluttering, his breathing shallow. She shook him gently. There was no response. She tapped his shoulder more firmly. "Sir... you have to leave the train". Nothing. She quickly radioed the station supervisor who without hesitation called for an ambulance.

The ambulance was there in eight minutes. The senior paramedic, a large middle-aged woman, felt for a pulse in the man's carotid artery. His eyes were open, his pupils dilated. There was no pulse. He was now clinically dead. She unbuttoned his vest, tore open his shirt as her young male colleague prepared the defibrillator and handed her the paddles. "Clear," she said, and the shock was applied. The man's body convulsed but the only response was a seepage of blood from a small wound in his chest. "Again, clear." Another shock. The body heaved, and more blood came from the wound. A third time they tried. More blood. No response. She handed the paddles back to her colleague.

"This man cannot be revived and has passed away. It is now 12:53 am," she declared. "Call the police. Nobody touches anything. This might be a crime scene." The young paramedic used his ambulance radio to request that the police attend a suspicious death.

CHAPTER TWO

Detective Inspector Robin Lazelle was a thirty-year veteran homicide investigator. For forty-five years he had been in the Victoria Police Force. Now aged sixty-three he was eligible for retirement. At the beginning of every case, he gave everyone around him the firm impression that his involvement was a huge personal inconvenience. His demeanour at crime scenes was mostly curt with limited conversation. He could be considered grumpy if he said anything much at all. This became exaggerated in the small hours of the morning.

His Detective Sergeant, Barry (Baz) Kellogg, knew him well enough by now to indulge his boss. They had been partnered for three years. Word about the squad room was that Lazelle had put some of the higher ranks in the police force offside because they thought that he was not a team player. He would often do things alone against the express protocol that detectives should work in pairs with the second officer recording in a notebook all that was said. At the same time, Lazelle was admired and considered almost indispensable because of his clear focus and analytical skills.

His boss, the Head of Homicide, Detective Superintendent Charles Pizzey, let him do things his own way. As the 'Super' often claimed, "he may not be a people person but he can certainly find the bad guys." His investigation results and subsequent convictions looked good for the Homicide Squad.

Lazelle and Kellogg arrived on the scene at Hurstbridge around forty-five minutes after the paramedics had declared the passenger dead. In the station car park an ambulance, two Divisional police vans and three other cars all had flashing lights activated. In the waiting room, the Station supervisor, train driver and four uniformed police were gathered. The uniformed officers had proceeded to secure the scene and when Lazelle entered the carriage, a forensic scientist, crime scene photographer, the pathologist and her attendant were there. Upon his arrival all gathered ceded his authority at once to lead the case and take over. Such was the reputation of the successful homicide detective.

The pathologist, Dr Kristin McClelland, had examined the body. "He has been stabbed in the chest with the narrowest of weapons," she told Lazelle. "I think we'll find that has brought on heart failure or he has bled out internally. Not much blood has escaped his body".

"How long has he been dead?" asked Lazelle.

"I think he expired just before the ambulance arrived. Probably an hour ago, perhaps a little more," she answered. "The weather's mild, and rigor hasn't started."

The photographer finished and left the carriage. The forensic officer signalled he was done dusting for prints and moved aside for Lazelle. Without touching anything at first, he looked over the scene. There were no signs of any struggle or distress. No discarded papers. No rubbish. All very clean. There was no briefcase or carry bag as one might expect of an apparent businessman. The victim was seated exactly as he was found and untouched except for the open shirt. With gloved hands, Lazelle pulled the shirt aside and confirmed the wound was extremely small with just a little seepage of blood brought on by the resuscitator shocks. Without that tell-tale sign this might have been declared a sudden heart attack.

He checked the jacket and felt the inside pockets, then the waistcoat and trouser pockets. No wallet, no phone, no ID, only a Myki train pass in his outside jacket pocket. Lazelle concluded the passenger had used the train pass to tap on at the entry station and probably dropped it into his outside pocket to conveniently access and tap off at his destination. Had the businessman been carrying anything else, it was missing.

"You can take the body now," he told the pathologist. "I'll attend the autopsy say, 10:30 am tomorrow?" She nodded in agreement.

Back on the station platform, Baz Kellogg talked to the station supervisor and driver. Though they would be required to make formal statements, their position was straightforward. Neither knew the man nor had seen him at any stage before. Their role was purely one of discovery.

"We'll need to examine the carriage CCTV to find out where he got on the train and who else was in the carriage," said Kellogg.

Lazelle grunted an affirmative response then added, "and when you establish the vision of him coming into the carriage, check the CCTV around that station including the street monitors, not just the Metro cameras."

And with that the older man waved his hand as if to dismiss all assembled and walked away to his car for the drive home.

It was already 9:15 am and Lazelle had overslept. The alarm he set on his phone was never going to wake him as he must have switched it to silent when he arrived at the crime scene.

He regarded himself in the mirror... unshaven, bushy eyebrows, jagged jaw line, a few more wrinkles than he had noticed before. His hair was receding and grey, the years were showing. He stood 178 centimetres tall... probably a couple of centimetres less than in his youthful days. With age the body had shrunk in height but not so overall. He was now bulging in the midriff and could be described as 'solid' or even 'stocky'.

His unit was in a single-level ground floor building, entry hall, kitchen, and family room, two bedrooms, one bathroom and a study. When he and his wife Jane had downsized, they were particularly attracted to this place because of the Tasmanian oak cathedral ceiling in the main living area, and the use of the same wood for numerous inbuilt shelves there and in the study. They enjoyed the natural look that came with wood. It felt warm and inviting. It also complemented their walnut sideboard where in the glass cases were displayed fine China plates, a silver coffee set, crystal decanters, wine and whisky glasses and special figurines. On the sideboard was a selection of Scotch whiskies.

The family room had a mahogany dining table and six matching chairs with old world tapestry seats. The long settee was piled high with cushions that had to be moved if someone wanted to sit there. Then there was his favourite reclining black leather chair near the gas fireside. Jane always said it looked out of place. Wrong colour. Didn't match the tastefully decorated, well-furnished living room. However, his chair was his indulgence. He loved to relax and think there.

In the bedrooms the headboards were rosewood and the beds piled high with pillows and cushions. Again, you had to throw cushions off the beds to use them. Around the rooms were framed family photographs. Everything was still in place exactly as she would have wanted. It was an exceptional effort for a man who had lived alone since he lost Jane to cancer four years ago.

He showered, shaved, and changed into his work attire, grey tailored trousers with a brown belt, business shirt, maroon tie, a blue jacket, grey socks, and comfortable slip-on tan leather shoes. Unlike his younger colleagues, who would dress more casually, Lazelle maintained the dress standard, just as he was used to when he was promoted to be a detective 30 years ago.

It was late August, near the end of winter. Springtime was just around the corner. The sun was shining and the temperature comfortable, at least temporarily as the forecast was for rain and a cold afternoon. By eleven o'clock he was at the forensic science lab in the mortuary with Dr McClelland. She had already opened the body and began showing Lazelle what the stab wound had done.

"The instrument was consistently thin like a length of firm wire. It has easily slipped between the ribs near the sternum and penetrated the anterior lobes of the heart in the right ventricle. The wound is 20 centimetres long." She paused to allow Lazelle time to understand. He was usually quick to comprehend but this morning he looked tired and out of sorts. A lack of sleep, she thought.

"Could he have fallen on a spike?" he asked.

"Maybe… but the body falling would almost certainly have bent the implement. This wound is straight all the way like the wire has been driven into his body."

Lazelle waited for her to continue.

"The puncture of the heart is so small that when the heart muscle contracts to pump blood through the arteries it seals the wound. Only when the heart relaxes does it bleed. There is a strong possibility that this man survived for more than an hour as he gradually bled out. He would have within say, fifteen minutes suffered hypotension, low blood pressure and fallen unconscious. From what I understand the paramedics found him just after he died and could not revive him."

"Why didn't he seek help?" the detective asked.

"It is very likely he didn't know he'd been stabbed," she replied.

CHAPTER THREE

Georgina Christodoulou was the technical member of the squad. They all called her Georgie, and she was the bubbly life and soul of the team. She had been recently married in a strict Greek Orthodox Church wedding to a man from another family of the same faith. The whole team attended the church service and all but Lazelle went on to the lavish reception and acquitted themselves passably well with their 'Zorba' dancing. Lazelle handed his gift to the bride's mother at the church and excused himself from attending the celebrations.

Georgie and Baz Kellogg began watching the Metro Rail CCTV from the start of the train's journey at 11:04 pm from Flinders Street, through the city loop and there was no sign of the victim. At North Richmond station, he entered the carriage. He was walking normally, carrying a small backpack and sat in the seat where he was eventually found.

At that late hour there were just five other single travellers, four men and a woman spread out farther down the carriage. Two men were intently looking at their phones and another had earphones and was probably listening to music. The fourth man was apparently asleep, the middle-aged woman just relaxed, arms folded and leaning back in her seat.

At Victoria Park three youths all dressed alike with jeans, identifiable T-shirts and baseball caps worn at various angles and one back-to-front, joined the carriage and sat nearby laughing. Though there was no sound on the tape, obviously they were boisterous and intoxicated. Only the woman seemed to observe them.

The victim by now had his head rested against the window and seemed fast asleep. The youths began to focus on him and one, the guy with the baseball hat on backwards, and with a Chicago Bears T-shirt, moved next to him. He apparently spoke to the man without any response. He nudged the man to wake him but still no reaction. After that he passed the backpack across to the other two youths, felt inside the man's jacket pocket and took a wallet which he threw to the others. He patted down the other pockets and took nothing more. They left the train at Darebin station.

Immediately after the youths got off the train, the woman approached the man and tried to wake him. She had witnessed the robbery. He gave no response. For several minutes she kept on nudging him. Vision showed her speaking to him. Nothing. She gave up and left the train at Heidelberg.

Lazelle arrived and they showed him the video. The camera angle was front on with a clear view of the youth taking the bag and wallet. The victim was unconscious and there was no evidence of any attack.

"His phone must have been in the backpack," said Lazelle. "When we identify him, we can perhaps trace the phone. Have we asked for the CCTV locations around North Richmond Station?"

"Yes," said Georgie. "I'll have it within the hour."

"The woman in the train… she saw what was happening. We must find her and see what she has to say. Release that carriage CCTV footage to the media for the news at 6:00 pm tonight. Talk about a robbery and don't mention his death. If we can have these youths identified quickly it may help us some," said Lazelle.

Then he added, "and show the vision of the woman and ask her to come forward."

"Yes Sir," said Georgie.

Lazelle went back to his desk and Kellogg joined him.

"The postmortem shows he was stabbed by something like a firm piece of wire leaving a very small entry wound. The implement pierced the heart, and it bled out slowly," he told his sergeant. "I guess we must consider if it could have been an accident? Did he fall on something? That seems unlikely. The postmortem suggests that the direct straight wound of near 20 centimetres long into his heart was a deliberate stabbing. So, we must assume the attack was with the intention of doing bodily harm. Theft was not the motive, as we have just witnessed three drunk young kids opportunistically robbing him. The victim was unconscious at the time."

The additional community CCTV footage came and was examined carefully. It was a clear night, and you could see the victim walking into North Richmond Station from the east. Cameras further down the street had him leaving St. Barts Hospital through the main entrance at 11:05 pm. He's out of any camera surveillance for five minutes from 11:07 until he arrives at the station at 11:12, swipes his Myki card and drops it into his side pocket. Vision shows him sit down and place his hand on his chest. He stands up a little unsteadily and boards the train at 11:17.

By late morning, Lazelle and Kellogg were at the large public hospital and they showed the photo of the dead man to the receptionist. The young woman on the desk didn't know him but suggested they see Associate Professor Lucille Sloane, CEO of the St. Barts Hospital Foundation. She was located nearby in an office purposely positioned in the foyer to be accessible to the public for donations, the sale of used books, badges, hats, scarves, and other fundraising paraphernalia.

"Lucy has been here forever," said the receptionist.

They entered the Foundation Office and waited for a few minutes while Prof. Sloane finished up another meeting.

"Come into my office," she said warmly. "What can I do for the police?"

"We are trying to identify this man," Kellogg handed her the photograph.

"Oh, that's Dr Francis Grace," she said immediately. "He's an anaesthetist attending here at St. Barts."

"Who can tell us what he was doing yesterday?" asked Lazelle. "He left the hospital very late and caught a train home."

Prof. Sloane picked up the telephone and dialled. A few seconds later she asked, "Rupert, what surgery was on yesterday that Doc Grace was involved in?" She paused for the answer, thanked the person, and put down the phone.

"That was head of surgery and he said Doc Grace was the anaesthetist for a long emergency heart operation that started at 5:30 pm yesterday afternoon. The cardiac surgeon was Mr Johannes Van der Merwe. He and Doc Grace have teamed up for many operations over the past few years. What has happened?" she asked.

Lazelle declined to answer. "I need Dr Grace's home address please."

CHAPTER FOUR

It was just after midday when Lazelle and Detective Constable Samantha (Sam) Long called at the Grace family Eaglemont home.

Dr Grace's wife Anne looked exhausted and was dressed in loose-fitting casual clothes. He doubted she had been to bed. She was a brunette with shoulder-length hair, of medium height and average build. Lazelle thought she could be a very attractive woman in better circumstances.

Their home was a beautiful two-storey house with all the attendant luxuries, pool, patio, four bedrooms, upstairs and downstairs bathrooms, large lounge and family rooms, beautifully modern kitchen with Italian marble benchtops and high-end appliances... a multi-million-dollar price tag.

She invited Lazelle and Long to be seated in the lounge and sat opposite them.

"What has happened to my husband?" she asked.

"I am sorry to say I have bad news," said Lazelle. "Your husband was found on a train in the railyards at Hurstbridge early this morning. I am afraid he had passed away."

Mrs Grace was at first shocked, put her hands to her face, appeared to almost faint then after a few seconds burst into tears sobbing uncontrollably. Sam moved to sit next to her and put her arm about the widow. Lazelle sat silent.

After what seemed like a very long time, he said, "I am sorry to tell you that this was not a natural death. It appears his heart had been pierced by a thin implement. Perhaps he might have had a fall and there was a spike nearby... but we must also consider that he may have been attacked by somebody using a weapon."

The wife continued to sob softly. They waited. She wiped her eyes with a tissue and daintily blew her nose. When she was a little more composed Lazelle continued.

"May I ask you a few questions Mrs Grace? I realise this is a difficult time for you but the sooner we can find some answers the better."

"I'll try," she said.

"Can you tell me what you know of your husband's movements since you last saw him?" asked Lazelle.

"He was rostered for surgery during the day. Then he told me he was involved in an emergency cardiac operation that would go late. His phone was always out of reach during these critical times. I contacted the hospital at midnight to ask about the surgery. At first no one could help me. It was another twenty minutes before I was transferred to the nurses' station in intensive care and I was told the patient involved was brought there at 11:15 pm.

"By then it was 1:00 am. The trains had stopped running. I telephoned Francis several times without any answer. Then I called the police at 1:30 am. They assured me that they would follow up with a missing person's report. I called them twice again this morning only to be told that the matter was still under investigation."

"Why was he on the train? Why didn't he drive to St. Barts... the doctors all have car parking," he asked.

"Francis preferred train travel and hated driving in traffic jams. He often said he had time to think on the train. He came from Oxford, was British to the core, never mind now being in Australia. Britons caught trains, he always said."

"We have CCTV footage that shows your husband being robbed by some youths on the train while he was unconscious. We believe the injury was done before and he didn't even realise it. It doesn't seem like a random act. Do you know of anyone he was having trouble with?"

"Not really," she considered the question tearfully. "No. He was a quiet, reserved man. He didn't have many friends and I doubt he had any enemies."

"How did he get on with his colleagues… the people he worked with?"

"I really don't know. He was always tired and left his work behind at the hospital. The one person he probably knew best was a fellow anaesthetist, Dr Garry Johnson. If there is anything to find out about their work, you should ask him. So far as our personal lives are concerned, we tend to stay in our own circle of friends and family."

She started to break down again. "Please, I am not sure I can answer anything sensibly right now… I'm sorry. This has been such a terrible shock." She began to cry quietly. Sam handed her more tissues.

"Do you have children?" he asked.

"Two daughters… they are at school now. I don't know how I will tell them …" her voice choked, and she sobbed. Sam held her one free hand in both of hers. Lazelle could see that the young detective was feeling emotional too.

"Do you have other family here in Melbourne?"

"Yes, my mother and father."

"Call your parents to come over and DC Long will stay with you until they arrive. She can help explain what has happened. And may I suggest that your parents should be here when your daughters come home from school. Thank you for your assistance, and we are so sorry for your loss."

Lazelle left the Grace home, stepping outside into what had now become an overcast, cold and rainy day. Telling a family member that a loved one had just been killed was a difficult and sensitive moment even for a seasoned detective. Lazelle felt about as bleak as the weather. He could only imagine the moment Grace's daughters would be told that their father wasn't coming home.

He remembered his own sadness as a thirteen-year-old boy when his young sister, Cathy died aged eleven. Words mean little to a child, when talking about the death of a loved one that leaves the child's heart broken.

He remembered his family and the long ship voyage when they emigrated from England on the Australian ten-pound scheme in 1968. He was 8 and Cathy 6 when they arrived in Melbourne. He felt that they, as a new immigrant family, were very different. So, they remained socially withdrawn in public and at home. They didn't fit in.

His sister Cathy was profoundly deaf. They all learned to sign, and most family communications were soundless. Consequently, Robin Lazelle grew up in a quiet house. They barely talked. He was used to being withdrawn, lost in his own thoughts.

Cathy passed away aged 11 from a brain tumour that apparently had been latent and a reason for her early deafness. The family was devastated. Even though Cathy was gone, his mother would not speak to them and continued to sign. Their home remained silent except for the few occasions when he and his father would speak. That never happened in his mother's presence. It wasn't often. His father had little to say. And habitually the boy preferred to sign in his family home.

Lazelle reached his car. He paused, sadly remembering those days. Touching his heart, and pointing to the sky he signed, "I miss you, Cathy. I love you. God bless."

CHAPTER FIVE

Lazelle and Kellogg met Dr Garry Johnson mid-afternoon in a small meeting room, not at St. Barts, but at a private hospital where the anaesthetist was rostered that day. A hospital orderly brought them coffee. They introduced themselves as detectives from the Homicide Squad.

"What is this about?" asked Dr Johnson.

"I am sorry to inform you that your colleague Dr Francis Grace was found dead in a train last night."

Johnson was shocked. "What happened?" he asked. "Why are you involved?"

"At this stage we are investigating what appears to be a sudden death... it is a routine enquiry," said Lazelle. "We are always called in to assess any unusual situation like this."

"How can I help?"

"His widow, Anne, told us that amongst all of his colleagues, you probably knew him best. I wonder if you could tell us about him? And if you don't mind, it is standard practice for my colleague to take some notes. If you wish, we will provide you with a copy of that record."

The Doctor nodded his assent and began.

"Francis Grace was a very competent anaesthetist. I think he had just turned forty-seven a few months back. So, he is... excuse me... was... at the peak of his professional career with over twenty years' experience. I know he worked at a top London hospital before coming to Australia. We respected one another, and I suppose, it is true that he was closer to me professionally than anyone else."

"How long had he been working at St. Barts?"

"He had been in Australia for about ten years. We anaesthetists tend to team up with surgeons. Sometimes, they work at different hospitals, so we follow their rosters. Francis worked with three or more surgeons, mainly at St. Barts. And he was also on a regular roster with the Emergency Department in case of any urgent surgery. So, he worked pretty well full-time at St. Barts."

"Did Dr Grace have any enemies.... can you think of any trouble he may have had?"

Johnson thought for a moment. Lazelle waited and did not hurry him.

"Not really. He was so low-key and such a loner that he was never really in the limelight. The only time was..." the doctor paused wondering if he should say more.

"What do you mean... the only time?"

"It was so long ago. Really it can't be important now."

"It might be. What happened?" asked Lazelle.

"St. Barts is a major hospital and has a mixture or private and public patients. Early in his time at St. Barts, Francis embarrassed himself at a surgical team meeting. It was a regular quarterly meeting of hospital administrators, surgeons, anaesthetists, perfusionists and senior theatre nurses where we would review cases and examine the surgical procedures. It wasn't so much a clinical meeting. More a time where the hospital administration was on the lookout to save money by doing things better and faster and cheaper. I might add, better and cheaper is usually a contradiction in terms.

"Francis was quiet and never said much. That's why what happened really stood out and shocked everyone. He became very angry, voice raised and entirely out of character. He chastised almost everyone in the room about the hospital's priorities for surgery. Coming out of the NHS in the United Kingdom where all services were free, he was uncomfortable with the way we would provide almost immediate surgical procedures to patients with private health insurance. The private cases generated more income for the hospital and the doctors. He was annoyed that we had to waitlist public patients covered only by our national Medicare that paid the hospital less. In a lot of cases these public patients' surgeries were just as urgent and some were delayed for many, many months.

"One particular case had especially upset Francis. This was a woman in her late forties who needed a hip replacement and she had waited for almost two years. It was an unusual combination of the family doctor not urgently referring her, the orthopaedic surgeon having personal problems and taking time off. When he returned to work, he was unwilling to fit her in ahead of his more lucrative private patients who had been waiting for him as well.

"Francis berated the hospital administration for not allocating enough beds for public cases. He slammed the surgeon for allowing it to happen… the patient's leg had withered so badly waiting for the surgery that by the time the hip was replaced it was going to be very difficult to rehabilitate her to be able to walk again properly, if at all. The delay probably was the difference between a normal recovery and possibly ending up in a wheelchair.

"He was the anaesthetist at her operation. He heard talk about the case that upset him during the surgery but didn't say anything then because he would never have distracted the procedure. The 'blow up' came the very next week and that just happened to be our regular quarterly surgical team meeting. Francis never worked with that surgeon again.

"Though his point was probably valid, he had perhaps unwisely used some very strong language, calling us colonial pretenders and saying that we wouldn't last two minutes practising real medicine in Britain. Rubbish of course. In the British NHS they waitlist urgent surgeries all the time. But for Francis, who did not talk much, to suddenly lash out at us all and call us second rate medical practitioners... well, he became labelled as the typical "whingeing Pom". He made no friends in the room that day.

"He never apologised. Others kept him at a distance. Francis didn't seem to care and wanted nothing personal to do with almost everyone. As I said, I was probably closest to him because as a colleague, I made time for him. Not social... but professional time, maybe sometimes over coffee or a sandwich. We never spoke of the incident again."

Lazelle let the silence dwell for a moment.

"Do you think that the incident, as you put it, led to any real long-term bad feelings? Does anyone care now?"

"Probably not. There's no talk about it now. It was eight years ago, so perhaps forgotten by those still here. And of course, today we have many new team members who were not part of that meeting," Johnson added. "But whatever ill-will remained, Francis brought upon himself. He didn't care to strike up any friendships. He didn't care what others thought. He just did his job. And to be honest, we work long hours. We work in teams that are thoroughly professional. We go home to families who hardly ever see us, tired and short of sleep to get up the next day and do it all again. There's no time for group hugs."

"Can you think of any recent problems he may have had?" asked Lazelle.

Johnson thought for a moment as if to decide whether he would say more. Then he shook his head. "No, there's nothing else."

CHAPTER SIX

The Victoria Police Homicide squad comprised some forty-eight members, thirty-six sworn police detectives, six consultants assigned full-time for their expert knowledge, and six lay administrative assistants. Though Criminal Investigation Divisional police may be called to crime scenes, any suspicious death, anywhere in Victoria, was immediately handed over to the Homicide Squad. Each case had its own dedicated team of detectives under the leadership of a Detective Inspector or an experienced Detective Sergeant. Uniformed police would be brought in to help for special duties if the workload overwhelmed the permanent numbers.

It was now 4:30 pm Thursday. Lazelle's team were gathered in the squad room. For this initial meeting, they were joined by Detective Superintendent Pizzey, Head of Homicide. There would be six working on this case. Detective Inspector Lazelle the leader, Detective Sergeant Kellogg his number two, assisted by Detective Senior Constable John Reed, and two Detective Constables, Sam Long and David Wells. And Georgie.

Baz Kellogg was mid-thirties and hoped to lead his own homicide investigations soon. He had worked through the ranks as a street cop to the Criminal Investigations Division and then seven years ago he was assigned as a Detective Constable to the Homicide squad. Lazelle had nominated him for promotion to Detective Sergeant and kept him as his right-hand man these past three years.

Detective Senior Constable John Reed was late fifties, and a gay man with a regular partner. He kept his body trim with a careful diet and exercise. At work he was all detail. He had been in the Homicide squad for over fifteen years and was considered a central character especially doing things by the book. He was a pleasant, engaging man, well-liked, and he enhanced the teamwork.

Detective Constable Sam Long was a star. Just 26 years old, she had been in Homicide for only eighteen months but was an outgoing, considerate person whose mind was razor-sharp. Lazelle favoured her in many situations and would take her with him instead of Kellogg for certain parts of any investigation.

Detective Constable David Wells was much the same age as Kellogg, mid-thirties though he looked much older. His hair was thinning and he was developing a bald spot. Whenever he showed any facial expression, he seemed puzzled. He was a "plodder" in police language and worked slowly and methodically.

Georgie was 29 years old, the 'go to' tech expert. She had been in the homicide squad for seven years, recruited as an outside lay IT and communications specialist. A lovely, if somewhat overweight woman, she sparkled and made everyone feel better. And she was brilliant with computers, cameras, enhancing images, dealing with the people at forensics and working with outside companies to find the evidence that helped solve cases. Her work also entailed checking Victoria Police records and the national database held by the Australian Federal Police. As names came to notice in any case, she would check out the people on the records and could have whatever information was available within the hour.

Lazelle addressed the group. "We are now day one in this investigation. We must be open to the idea that there may have been an accident and Dr Grace fell and was injured. But the pathologist, Dr McLelland and I both doubt it. The post-mortem shows the wound was straight, did not deviate and was 20 centimetres long. It hardly seems possible to fall onto a wayward spike, or fencing wire that does not bend or create a torn type of wound.

"I suspect we are investigating the carefully planned murder of a senior doctor at one of our major public hospitals. This might become a high-profile case and attract media attention. So, I want us to be very careful about what information we release in public. We will not say anything about murder... at present this is an investigation into a sudden death.

"Here's what we know. The victim is Dr Francis Grace, and he was the anaesthetist in an emergency operation performed by a team led by cardiac surgeon Johannes Van der Merwe that ended late Wednesday night at St. Barts Hospital.

"CCTV shows him leaving the hospital at 11:05 pm and walking west out of sight at 11:07. We have no vision from 11:07 until 11:12 when the railway CCTV shows him entering the precinct at North Richmond station, take out his Myki card from his wallet and 'tap on' for the train trip home. He places his wallet back in the inside pocket of his suit jacket. He drops the railcard into a side pocket. He has a backpack slung over his shoulder and at this stage is walking normally but slowly.

"He enters the station, sits down, and we see his hand feeling his chest apparently with some discomfort. He sits there for about 5 minutes until the train arrives. He clearly does not know he's been mortally injured. I feel this is very significant. He's a doctor and doesn't realise he has been stabbed... that suggests the attack was not at all obvious to the victim.

"At 11:17 he stands up a little unsteadily. He gets on the train and sits in the same seat where we found him deceased. He seems to be unconscious within ten minutes, because when the youths rob him, he is unable to be roused and that is at 11:28. The youths get off the train at the next stop to do a runner… that's Darebin at 11:31.

"The internal bleeding has lowered his blood pressure to the point that he passed out between 11:20 and 11:28. The actual time of death was in Hurstbridge just before the ambulance arrived around 12:40am. The wound was so small, the bleed out so slow, that he lasted more than an hour."

"I believe he was attacked in the side streets out of CCTV vision between the hospital and the station," Lazelle continued. "We need to call at all the houses in the streets he might have walked. DCs Long and Wells, you go doorknock. See if they saw or heard anything… see what they have in the way of private security vision.

"The television news tonight will show the footage of the robbery of a sleeping man on a train. And the woman we think witnessed the robbery. We will ask viewers to identify the youths and ask the woman to come forward. Hopefully we can retrieve his backpack and trace whatever his phone records might reveal.

"DSC Reed, you go to the hospital and find out about all the participants in the late-night emergency surgery. Get the details and arrange interviews for myself and DS Kellogg tomorrow."

Lazelle looked at them all in turn and asked, "Any questions?"

There were none.

CHAPTER SEVEN

It was 6 pm when they rang the doorbell at the Van der Merwe's house. It was a semi-detached Victorian building in East Melbourne, a lovely old home located near parklands and less than two kilometres from St. Barts Hospital.

A beautiful blonde, blue-eyed girl opened the door. She was in jeans and a T-shirt, with flip flops on her feet.

"Is Dr Van der Merwe home please?" asked Kellogg.

"Who may I say is calling?" she asked.

"We're Police detectives" he replied.

"Wait here." She closed the door.

After a few minutes a clean-shaven middle-aged man, dark hair, slim, well-groomed and good-looking, dressed in a collared shirt and Chino trousers and in bare feet, opened the door.

"Please come in," he stepped aside for them to enter. "I'm Johannes Van der Merwe." They both gave him their cards. In earlier days Lazelle had been paired with a colleague from Pretoria in South Africa. He knew Van der Merwe was a common Afrikaans surname. He could hear the unique accent.

They were seated in a very beautiful, expensively furnished lounge room. The surgeon asked, "How can I help you? It seems rather late for police to be knocking on my door. Is it about Dr Grace?"

Lazelle knew that the death of Dr Grace would already have become known within the hospital network because of their previous interviews with Dr Garry Johnson and Anne Grace. The surgeon had not read their cards identifying them from the Homicide Squad so Lazelle decided to ask questions without further explanations. "We understand he was with you in an emergency operation last night. How late did the surgery go, and do you have any idea about Dr Grace's movements afterwards?"

"It was a five-hour operation that started around 5:00 pm. We woke the patient up at maybe 10:15 and after changing out of our scrubs, we were both able to leave around 11 pm. Francis uses the train, so I guess he walked to the station."

"Did you see him leave?"

"No."

At that moment a woman entered the room. She was mid-thirties, maybe older, very beautiful, blonde hair, tall and slender and clearly related to the girl who answered the door. She could easily have been a model in the pages of Vogue. "Emmie, these gentlemen are detectives from the police. This is my wife, Emmie."

"Good evening," they both said in unison. "I am Detective Inspector Lazelle, and this is Detective Sergeant Kellogg. We are from the Homicide squad."

The surgeon remained very calm. His wife seemed horrified and blurted out, "What homicide. Who has been killed? What in God's name has happened?" She too had a heavy Afrikaans accent.

"Dr Grace was found dead at the end of the line in a train carriage early this morning. He never made it home. We believe he was robbed on the train and appears to have died from heart failure," Lazelle did not lie, but he did not mention the mortal injury.

"Why are you involved then?" asked the surgeon.

"All sudden deaths are subject to a post-mortem here in Victoria. In this case the pathologist found a puncture wound to the heart that bled out slowly causing hypotension and death."

Now the surgeon looked very concerned. "So, he had a heart attack on the train probably caused by the trauma of being attacked and robbed," he proffered.

"That's what we are trying to find out. What was your relationship like with Dr Grace?"

"Professional. Very professional always. He was my preferred anaesthetist."

"Did you detect any tension between any of the team members in surgery with Dr Grace?"

"Not at all. We've all worked together at St. Barts since I came here two years ago. Are you suggesting there was foul play?"

"Tell me about your background, please?" Lazelle ignored his question.

The surgeon was getting a little annoyed. "I'm not sure that has much to do with this but my wife and I and our two children, Colleen and Hansie, emigrated from South Africa. I was trained as a doctor at the University of Cape Town then I practised in the hospital system there."

"We will be speaking with each member of your operating team tomorrow," Lazelle responded. "As you are their leader, we thought it respectful to see you first tonight. Thanks for your time and again, I am sorry to be here at this hour and to give you such bad news about one of your colleagues. We will need to speak to you again after we have more information."

Both husband and wife saw them out.

Within an hour of the 6 pm evening news broadcast the police call line had identified the youth in the Chicago Bears T-shirt. The local CID picked up the thief. The youth quickly caved in and identified his mates. All three were arrested and detained at Heidelberg police station and Dr Grace's backpack, phone, and wallet were retrieved. The deceased man's possessions were rushed to Homicide HQ and delivered to Georgie.

Though it was now 9:00 pm, Lazelle and Kellogg went straight to the station to interview the youths. Heidelberg CID held them charged with robbery until the Homicide detectives arrived. None of them knew the man was dead. They only knew they had been spotted on the train CCTV robbing a sleeping passenger.

The main perpetrator with the Chicago Bears T-shirt and the back-to-front baseball cap, was the primary interest.

"Did you think the man was unconscious?" Lazelle asked.

"I tried to disturb him and if he had reacted, I would have simply asked if he was okay," replied the youth. "The fact that he was out to the world just meant easy pickings."

"Think hard boy, because this is important. Did you see him breathing, or hear him snoring... anything like that... signs of life?"

"No Sir... we were drunk, and this was just a lark."

"Okay, you need to deal with the local CID and put-up bail. I believe you will all face court charged with stealing," said Lazelle. "I'm a homicide detective. We found the man at the end of the line, and he was dead."

The boys were horrified and all at once blurted protestations of innocence. "We didn't hurt him Sir."

"We know that. The CCTV shows you did no more than steal his backpack, and his wallet. However, I would suggest you amuse yourselves in more honest ways in future."

CHAPTER EIGHT

On Friday morning, Lazelle and Georgie examined the contents of the victim's backpack. Nothing was unusual. Dr, Grace took his own lunch so there was a plastic container that seemed to have the remnants of a salad. He had a commercial plastic spring water bottle. There was a medical journal and a small black collapsible umbrella.

His wallet contained a Victorian driver's licence, some credit cards, and an old Lotto ticket he had not yet checked to see if there were any winnings. Whatever cash he might have had was gone. His phone was still there.

"Georgie, follow up on the phone records from Dr Grace's mobile," Lazelle instructed. "Also have the telecom company show where he has been in the past week. Search the Victorian and AFP data bases for any information about the Grace family."

Detective Constables Sam Long and Dave Wells had knocked on twenty doors in the side streets they predicted would be the most direct route from the hospital to North Richmond Station. Most were unanswered. They left prepared notes under the door asking the residents to contact them when they were home. The six residents they did speak with knew nothing that would help.

They rang the bell at the next door. It was answered by a young mother with obviously pre-school age children that they could hear carrying on in the background.

"Excuse us Ma'am. I am Detective Long, and this is Detective Wells. We believe a crime has been committed in this vicinity and wondered whether you heard anything this past Wednesday night?"

She looked at each of them thoughtfully. "Well, as a matter of fact my little girl had a bad dream and I was up with her around 11 pm when I heard a clatter outside," she said. "I looked out on the street from upstairs and I saw two people. A man had fallen on the ground and the other, a cyclist, was helping him up. I don't know what happened, but it seemed as though the cyclist had accidentally run into the pedestrian." She pointed to the place where it happened just across the road.

"What did you see next?" asked Wells.

"They seemed to be okay. The cyclist rode off and the other man started walking towards the train station."

"Can you describe them?"

"Not really. The cyclist was wearing what looked like a light three-quarter length raincoat and wore a helmet. I couldn't tell if it was a male or female. The man who had been on the ground seemed to be of average height, well-dressed, and I saw him attempt to clean up his clothes and dust himself off."

"Did you hear anything that was said?"

"No. There were no raised voices… it just seemed to be an accident. They were both well-mannered."

"Do you think they knew each other?"

"It's possible," she replied. "There are a lot of people working at the hospital near here and they are coming and going at all hours of the day and night."

"Does anyone around here have a security camera?" asked Sam Long.

"I really don't know," she said as one of the children screamed in the background. "Please. I must go."

Both detectives thanked the woman. They crossed the road and searched where the cyclist had hit the man. They looked for a spike on the footpath, or near the fence… anything that might have caused the dead man's injury by accident. There was nothing to find.

The woman on the train was named Dianne Brasher. She had contacted the police after seeing the TV news and made herself available Friday morning. After introducing themselves, the detectives sat with her in the interview room at Heidelberg Police station.

"Thanks for coming forward so soon,' said Kellogg. Lazelle had assigned his Sergeant to take the lead. "You were on the last Hurstbridge line train Wednesday night. Tell us what you saw."

Mrs Brasher was clearly nervous. "I saw the three youths get on the train. They were loud and drunk. I tried to keep to myself. After a short while the one with the hat on back-to-front sat next to the gentleman who was asleep. The boy nudged him and when there was no response, he took the man's things and gave them to the others."

"We saw all that on the train's CCTV. What happened when they left at Darebin Station?"

"I went over to the man to try and tell him he had been robbed but he was fast asleep. I couldn't wake him. I tried but he was unresponsive. When my stop came at Heidelberg, I left the train. I must say I felt uncomfortable at the time. I feel I should have called an ambulance."

Lazelle spoke. "Mrs Brasher, the man was mortally wounded during an incident before he got on the train."

"Do you mean he was found dead?" she asked, fearful that she had done something wrong.

"There was nothing you could have done. He was probably gone when you were trying to wake him. Thanks for talking with us."

Lazelle told a deliberate untruth to spare her feelings. There was a major public hospital across the road from Heidelberg station, and had the victim been found and attended to then he may have survived.

CHAPTER NINE

DSC Reed showed his Police ID at St. Barts reception. He was taken to the Human Relations Manager who provided the contact details of all persons involved with the emergency surgery Wednesday evening. HR contacted some of the team that were available that day and planned for the detectives to speak with them that afternoon. The others would be contacted and seen later.

Kellogg came to the hospital for the interviews. Reed was asked to join him and take notes.

The first person in the surgical team they would talk to was one of the theatre nurses, Alice Cook. After the introductions, they explained that Dr Grace had been found dead on the train. There was no mention of murder though they knew the widow and Dr Johnson had been informed of his suspicious death and word would travel fast. Surely many of his hospital colleagues would already know there had been foul play. Kellogg began the interview.

"Can you recall anything different during the surgery that night?"

"It was a tense time," she began. "The patient had a series of heart attacks here in the hospital and it was not a simple matter for stenting. Mr Van der Merwe had to do open-heart surgery to graft bypasses.

Usually a four-hour operation, but this took a little longer. He did three grafts. Otherwise, it was routine."

"Was Dr Grace his usual self?" asked Kellogg.

"I think so. He is reserved... a real Englishman, acted like royalty... so his involvement in discussion was mostly professional. He was never one to start a conversation and certainly, never became involved in anything argumentative."

"What sort of relationship did he have with Mr Van der Merwe?"

"He was his regular anaesthetist. They did not have a personal relationship that I know of. Distant I would say... maybe even tense at times. Others would just call it professional and nothing more."

"What do you mean?"

"I don't know how to describe it. In the last six months, it seemed to me as if Mr Van der Merwe had issues with him. Other than medical talk, Mr Van der Merwe would seem to deliberately try and annoy Dr Grace... for example the other night something came up and he asked in a sarcastic voice, "being passionate, what say you, Frankie?" He hated being called other than Francis... he was very conservative."

"Why did that happen?"

"The young surgical registrar was talking about his girlfriend, I think. He was joking about passion running hot and cold."

"Why would Van der Merwe ask a conservative Englishman about passion?"

"I think that's the point. Probably accusing him of having no feelings. Most of us can hardly imagine Francis Grace becoming animated let alone passionate."

The surgeon assisting in the late-night emergency procedure was Mr Raymond Goldstein. He was a Fellow of the Royal Australian

College of Surgeons, a renowned researcher at the Medical Research Institute attached to St. Barts. His research project was into the optimum temperatures required to preserve the heart muscle while on bypass, and the project had a reasonable Australian Government grant. Nevertheless, he liked to keep his surgical activity up to date and usually gave two sessions a week assisting other cardiac surgeons in mainly open-heart operations. He was well-credentialled and the leading surgeon always saw his involvement as a benefit. He was in his laboratory when the detectives called.

Kellogg began the interview. "What do you recall about the night of the operation?"

"It was normal, I think. The actual surgery ended up becoming a triple bypass, one more than we originally planned, but with the heart before us and another coronary artery looking problematic, we took some extra time to fix that as well. The patient is making a good recovery, I understand."

"Aside from the surgery and professional talk, did you notice anything personal happening in the room?"

"Not really. There's always chit-chat during the more mundane parts of the surgery. It might be small talk, usually amongst the nurses and sometimes between the surgeons, perfusionist and anaesthetist. It was unusual for Dr Grace to say much. To me he was extremely reserved, often unapproachable. Johannes would often speak up about this and that. He's been with us two years or so. He came from South Africa and in the early days of his tenure here he would compare our work to that of the Cape Town hospitals. They were very big in cardiac surgery there you know. Christiaan Barnard did the first ever heart transplant in the world at the Groote Schuur hospital where Van der Merwe was trained as a cardiac surgeon."

"What did he think of the standards here?"

"I think he thought this was a good place to work. In the beginning he would big note about what he had done back in Cape Town to establish himself here. But that faded as we all understood he was a very good cardiothoracic surgeon. He didn't need to tell us. We could see for ourselves."

"How did he and Dr Grace get on?"

"They were very professional. I don't think they had anything to do with one another outside of work."

Kellogg paused for a moment before asking. "Do you recall any terse comment made by the surgeon to Dr Grace during the operation?"

"Like what?" asked Goldstein.

"Something about 'passion'."

"Oh… that exchange… I would describe that as light-hearted… a bit of a joke. But remember we are all operating late night, unexpected surgery, tired and perhaps a little on edge. I saw nothing wrong with what was said."

"Who amongst the surgical team or here at the hospital might have any knowledge about the relationship between Van der Merwe and Grace?" asked Kellogg.

"The Charge Nurse would be the peacekeeper in these matters."

CHAPTER TEN

Charge Nurse Jenny Walker was a senior, maternal figure in the surgical rooms. All theatre staff and the surgeons respected her. Kellogg and Reed sat with her soon after.

"Are you aware of any rift between Mr Van der Merwe and Dr Grace?" asked Kellogg directly.

She looked uncomfortable, shifting in her seat and hands fidgeting, fingers nervously folding and straightening.

"Well... about six months ago, I was talking to Mr Van der Merwe one-on-one during preparations in the operating theatre. I think I was saying how good the surgical team is with his leadership... you know... me being proud to be with them sort of thing. He surprised me when he said something like 'looks can deceive'. Then he referred to the cool calm British member of our team being deceptive... that he was not what he appeared to be."

"Did he elaborate?"

"He did say something I remember very well. It seemed so out of character. He said, 'It's the quiet ones with closed minds that can do the most harm,' then he really ended the conversation."

"Who else amongst the team would know Dr Grace best?"

'The only relationship Grace had in that team was with the perfusionist. During operations they sat next to each other, he monitors vital signs, and she looks after oxygenating the blood supply to the body while the heart is stopped. They had more to say to one another during operations."

Kellogg and Wells were able to speak with the perfusionist, Denise Whitby. Though not a qualified medical practitioner, as a perfusionist she was trained separately to operate the heart bypass machines. They were experts in that science. She was around forty years old and had been doing this for several years.

Ms Whitby had heard the news and was shocked. Kellogg explained that the homicide detectives had to establish what happened since an incident occurred that night which may have caused his death. He said no more than that.

"I got on quite well with Dr Grace," she told them. "We obviously had an integrated professional job to do but I was probably the one of that surgical team who would occasionally have coffee or lunch with him. He was very conservative and didn't share much."

"Do you remember anything about that night in surgery that could help us?"

"Something happened a few months ago, I am sure. I don't know what, but he seemed to have lost respect for Johannes Van der Merwe as a person... nothing to do with his skill as a surgeon. During the operation there was a snide remark made by the surgeon towards Francis. It was to do with understanding emotions or passion or something like that."

"Can you remember exactly what was said?"

"Not really. The banter was going on between the registrar and the other surgeons and suddenly in quite clear tones that everyone could hear, Van der Merwe turned and said something like 'passion… what say you, Frankie?' Francis mumbled something that only I could hear, and it sounded like… 'morals of an alley cat.' I don't know what that meant, and he never said any more to me.

CHAPTER ELEVEN

In the Homicide squad a lot of time is spent doing routine tasks. However, it is when a homicide occurs that the stress and exhaustion suffered by so many detectives peaks. During the early stages of a murder investigation the team never takes much time off except for a few hours here and there to shower, change clothes, and grab some sleep whenever they can find the time. The first few days are critical. Those intense hours and the extreme emotions of finding, examining the body, dealing with the deceased's family, and asking difficult questions of those closest to the victim, all take their toll even with seasoned detectives. For some, this really affects their personal lives.

It was Saturday. Lazelle telephoned ahead and made an appointment for himself and Sam Long to visit Anne Grace again. They sat in the same room where the morning sun was streaming through the windows. She was dressed in casual but quite lovely and expensive clothes he thought. With make-up on and at least partially refreshed, she was indeed a beautiful woman. This was a much brighter day than Thursday when he had told her about her husband's death and of course then, she was so distraught that any further sensible questioning became difficult.

"How are you doing?' he gently asked.

"Not so good. It has turned our lives upside down," she answered referring to herself and their two daughters.

"Again, I am sorry. I need to ask you some more questions if you please."

She nodded affirmatively. "Do you know how it happened yet?" she asked.

"Not exactly... but we believe your husband was stabbed... we are treating this as a very suspicious death... possibly a murder case."

"Oh..." Anne Grace stared out the window. Lazelle gave her a moment then asked, "Tell me a little bit about yourself and your husband. How did you meet, and how long have you been married?"

"Seventeen years. I worked in the UK National Health System, and we met at a hospital function in London where we both had assignments. I was an Australian girl seeing the world. I had just ended a relationship with another man and Francis was extremely understanding and kind in a very conservative way."

"How long were you in the UK?"

"I was there for nearly eight years all told. I went when I was 26 years old, did all the usual tourist things. Then, I had a job as a special educator, met a man and thought it was serious, so I stayed much longer than I intended. He left me for another woman after we had virtually lived together for two years."

"When you first met your husband, what was he like?"

"He was a gentleman. Francis's great strength wasn't what he said but the way he listened and then in very few words he could put you at ease... he was always able to help me feel more comfortable about whatever was troubling me. Back then, I must confess, he helped me get over losing Jack and I probably married him on the rebound."

"What was your relationship with him like recently?" asked Lazelle.

"Oh, I suppose it was normal. After so long and with children to cope with and his work, we were certainly less emotionally involved," she said candidly. "He was 47 and I am 45. Our children are two girls. Abbie is now 11 and Josie is 7 years old. I had Abbie in London but desperately wanted to live back in Australia. I felt this was a better place for our children's future than living in England. We came back here ten years ago.

"Francis made the move here to please me I know. We have been okay, I guess, but his very conservative attitude and limited desire to involve himself, his aloofness, distanced us from friends socially. I think it distanced us in our own relationship too. Though he seemed settled he refused to become Australian. I just accepted this as normal."

"How are your girls doing?"

"They are both devastated in different ways. Abbie, being older, seems to be quietly grieving. She's like her dad and doesn't show emotion. But I know she is very upset, and she will keep it inside for way too long, I fear. Josie, being much younger, is crying a lot and talking about her feelings. That's a good thing. My own emotions are so topsy-turvy just now. I don't know whether to laugh or cry sometimes. I know Francis's passing is bad for us and yet sometimes I feel relieved. And that makes me feel very guilty. I feel like a bad mother. I wonder how I can do more for the girls."

"How was his relationship with the girls?" asked Lazelle.

"He was busy. Fatherhood was probably not top of his priorities. In fact, since we came to Australia with Abbie then had Josie here, I think he felt the girls were why he had to give up England. That might be unfair, but he was a reluctant father in many ways. Though he was never an outgoing and emotional sort of person, I feel the girls were blamed somewhere in the back of his mind. The girls would never think that. He was what he was to them. They knew no difference."

"Did you notice any changes in your husband's behaviour recently?" the detective asked.

"He was more withdrawn than usual. Stiff upper lip sort of behaviour. But recently, particularly in the last month or so, I felt there was something seriously troubling him. I asked about it, and he just said it was work-related."

"And what about his work?"

"He felt perpetually tired and overwhelmed by the workload. The health system in Victoria is under a lot of stress. The hospitals are not staffed to the right numbers and there is a shortage of health professionals. Wait lists for elective and non-urgent surgery are long. The hospitals want their theatres occupied, so it is true he seemed to be involved in never-ending surgical procedures for very long hours."

"Did he mention any problems with colleagues or staff at the hospital?"

She looked out the window the sun shining a light in her eyes. "Going back many years he was very angry with the hospital administration and surgical colleagues because of patient waiting list times. There were cross words that he told me made him very unpopular. That's all he said. That was way back at the start."

"What about his relationship with the surgeon Van der Merwe?"

"In the past few months, he seemed to be seriously unhappy with Mr Van der Merwe. They had worked together ever since that family had landed from South Africa about two years ago. At first, he was satisfied with it all being a thoroughly professional relationship. He was a good surgeon, Francis told me."

"How did you know he was unhappy with Van der Merwe?" asked Lazelle.

"About six months ago, he told me that they had dinner at his place one evening after surgery. I believe the Van der Merwe's have a home nearby in East Melbourne. Francis took a break there before going back to the hospital for an eight o'clock meeting with some other colleagues. I am not sure what it was about, anaesthetics I think...

some sort of meeting with colleagues to work out what the hospital budget for their side of things should be."

"What happened at dinner?"

"He wouldn't tell me exactly. Just said it opened his eyes to the man. That is Francis all over, judging behaviour in others by his own imagined strict British standards. After that dinner he just said they worked professionally but he did not respect the man. He wouldn't elaborate."

"Do you work?"

"Yes. I volunteer two days a week at the Victorian Deaf Institute. I work with deaf children."

"That is close to my heart," Lazelle volunteered. Then with his hands he signed, "Can you sign?"

"Yes," she signed. "How did you become involved with deaf children?"

"My sister Cathy was deaf. She was two years my junior and died when I was thirteen."

"I'm sorry," she signed touching her heart.

"How did you learn to sign?" he signed.

"My work. I was qualified as a teacher for deaf children. My job here in Australia and then when I went to London was with deaf children. Mainly teaching signing to the very little ones or older kids that had become deaf."

Sam Long, who was busy taking notes was amazed to see her boss doing this. Her eyes wide open and pencil poised, she asked, "did either of you communicate anything I should note?"

Lazelle smiled. So did Anne Grace. "Sam, no. I was just explaining that my sister was deaf and in my family we all learned to sign." He turned to Mrs Grace. "How many days do you volunteer at the Institute?" They were speaking now.

"Just two days a week from 10 am to 3 pm, Wednesdays and Thursdays. All my other time is taken up being a mum. The children before and after school. By day there are household chores and grocery shopping. My social life is mundane... I have my parents in Melbourne, they are getting older, so I try to visit them each week. They come here to see the kids some weekends. I have some friends among the other school parents. We sometimes arrange to meet for coffee after school drop off. Most mums will tell you they don't have much time to be idle."

"I must ask this question and I realise it might seem offensive. In these recent times where you say there was a lack of emotional involvement, was there any other romantic interest?"

Anne Grace seemed startled. She was surprised by the question.

"What do you mean? she asked.

"Do you think your husband had any romantic interest outside your marriage?"

Lazelle noticed a fleeting moment of relief in her eyes.

"No. To be honest he was not a romantic person. Our love life was minimal."

"How did you feel about that?" he asked.

"I took it for granted and in Francis's case he was not a typical male."

Lazelle let that comment slide... he imagined her view of the typical male relentlessly searching for sexual gratification... a concept that had seemed to have passed him by long ago, and now at his age, without a wife, never considered.

"Could I please have the names and contact details of your parents and any of your friends who knew you and your husband? We'll wait if you would write them down for me."

She left the room and after a few minutes returned with a handwritten list. "Of all the names Sonia Baker is my closest friend," she said.

CHAPTER TWELVE

It was a beautiful Saturday afternoon. The sun was shining, sky clear and temperature pleasant. Football teams were playing on many sporting grounds throughout the city. Typically, Melbourne weather was difficult to forecast. You might have all four seasons in the one day. Certainly, today was a complete change from the wet and overcast conditions of the past two days.

Lazelle telephoned and arranged to visit Anne Grace's parents with Sam Long. Mr and Mrs Liddell lived in a modest home situated in Pascoe Vale, a northern suburb of Melbourne. He guessed they were both in their late sixties, maybe seventies, and retired. Mr Liddell had been a plumber for the whole of his working life and she a part time worker but mainly a stay-at-home wife and mother.

Anne was the elder of two daughters. They missed her terribly when she lived and worked in England. They had managed to find the money to attend her wedding to Francis Grace. Anne had visited them on another occasion during her eight years away. They were very pleased when she came home to Australia especially with baby Abbie, their first grandchild.

They sat in a small living room at the dining table. Sam took notes.

"Thank you for seeing us at such short notice," said Lazelle. "I am the detective leading the investigation into your son-in-law's death. I'd like to ask you a few questions if I may?"

The elderly pair nodded their assent. "It's a terrible thing," said Mrs Liddell.

Lazelle continued. "It is normal during a homicide investigation to try to understand the family dynamics of the deceased person. How would you assess the marriage of your daughter and Dr Grace?"

"It seemed to be normal enough," said Mrs Liddell.

"What did you think of your son-in-law?"

The father jumped in immediately and interrupted his wife. "I didn't think much of the man. From day one when we met him at the wedding all those years ago, he struck me as aloof, cold, and entirely unsuitable for my daughter. We have always been a working-class family, close and able to share with each other. We could talk. We could comfort one another when we needed to. We had feelings. We were what I consider to be a normal family.

"Francis was not normal. He was a 'cold fish'. I have no idea how my daughter could have become attracted to him. In the past several years, she has struggled to relate to him at all. At least that's my view. She only stayed with him to provide a family experience for the kids. But when the grandchildren are with us, it's plain they love their mother, but the concept of loving their father is mere words not feelings. He does nothing to earn the love of his children. I don't think he does anything with them."

All of this was said straight to the point and with the raw feelings you would expect of an honest, no-nonsense, working-class man.

Lazelle stayed silent, feeling that more would be said without him asking.

Mrs Liddell made the excuse. "The family is comfortable and well provided for by a specialist doctor who makes a lot of money. The children go to private schools, and they live luxuriously in a beautiful home. They are wealthy. We didn't have such privileges, so I think it is hard for us to understand the way a busy doctor's family relates to one another. My husband is right though. There's not the love and support the way we knew it. Anne would never say so, but when she was with us alone and could talk, she seemed unhappy, and she often made excuses for Francis being remote and consumed by his work."

"Do you have any ideas about who would want to harm your son-in-law?"

"No. We were not close to him." With that Mr Liddell was done talking and rose to make some tea.

"Your daughter mentioned she had a relationship with another man before Dr Grace. Can you tell me anything about that?"

"We never met the man. It was early in the time she was in London, and I had the impression that it was serious for her and she was extremely sad when it ended. I know Francis helped her to get over it all."

Lazelle had heard enough and thanked them for their help.

At five in the afternoon Lazelle arranged to meet Sonia Baker, the closest of the friends Anne Grace had listed. Sam Long went with him.

"Have you spoken to Mrs Grace about the death of her husband?" he asked.

"Yes. She called me soon after she knew, and we spoke. She said Francis had been murdered. Is that true?"

"How is she coping?" asked Lazelle, ignoring the question. He wanted as little as possible said about murder at this early stage of the investigation.

"Of course, it is a shock and there will be huge adjustments for her and the girls," Sonia replied.

"Did you ever have any social interaction with Dr Grace?"

"My husband and I had them to our place for dinner a couple of times and they reciprocated. It was never what I would call a great night for us. Francis was anti-social at best and his silence downright rude. The dinners never went late, and even a few glasses of wine never loosened up the conversation. The real relationship was between Anne and me. We would meet after school drop off and have coffee at least once every week."

"How would you assess her marriage?"

"Why are you asking this?" Sonia seemed uncomfortable being asked such a question. "Surely you should be trying to find out what happened, not worrying about their domestic situation."

"We always try to understand the family of the deceased. It helps us to know more about the victim and how he was thinking. That can lead us to find the person who did this," Lazelle answered. "In your coffee breaks did she speak about her personal life?"

"She was a good wife and good mother. She enjoyed her voluntary role at the Deaf Institute. She never said so, but I thought she was very unhappy with Francis. He had always been remote, but in the past few months he was even more distant. She confided in me that there was no intimacy… no sex life."

"Do you think there was someone else?" he asked. He was referring to Dr Grace and was surprised when Sonia immediately answered about Anne.

"I am not sure, but I certainly had the feeling Anne had found male company in some way or another. Francis was never home."

"Why do you say that?"

"In a recent conversation I cheekily said I couldn't do without sex, and I wondered how she coped. She smiled and said something about being a cougar."

"Did she give any detail?"

"No names. However, I think he was young. I'm not sure you know this but the whole cougar reference is all about an older woman being with a younger lover."

"I am aware of that," said Lazelle with a wry smile. "When did this conversation happen?"

"I reckon about three weeks ago. Let's not make too much of this. It was probably said in fun. Might have been flirting. Might have been her imagination. She was in a difficult position with that husband of hers."

"What young men would be around her?"

"I have no idea. They have a gardener to cut lawns and keep things tidy. There's a pool guy. Who knows? Maybe she took a fancy to someone delivering pizza. She didn't say more than that one cougar reference. Mostly we talked about our kids."

Lazelle ended the interview and at that late hour on the weekend asked Sam Long to organise school time surveillance of Anne Grace starting Monday. School hours without the children would be the only opportunity for any liaison to happen.

CHAPTER THIRTEEN

Kellogg had spent most of Saturday at St. Barts. He viewed the limited CCTV footage in the garage at the hospital, hoping to spot a cyclist like the one described by the witness of the accident with a pedestrian. Discussions so far with the parking attendants established that CCTV security could not identify cyclists. The cars of course all had registration plates and there was no trouble telling who came and went in a motor vehicle. Most of the senior hospital workers had predesignated parking bays. Others had to find a spot in the public car parking sections. But bikes just slid past the parking boom gates and were usually locked into a rack near the elevators to the main foyer and the upper medical wards and theatres.

Kellogg assigned four uniformed police officers, in two shifts, to interview all hospital cyclists around the clock. Each cyclist who entered the garage would be stopped and asked for identification. Their work at the hospital would be noted and a phone number and email address collected. Their movements on the night of the death were also noted. If the cyclist had left the hospital in the time frame of the assault their alibis were checked immediately. Georgie had given each policeman a notebook computer and the details collected were entered into a central file so that as cyclists came and went, duplications of any records could be eliminated. And Georgie would check out each entry as it happened.

When Baz Kellogg arrived home around 9:00 pm his wife, Jennifer was already in bed watching television. He was greeted by a stony silence and decided to shower and change before being confronted with whatever the problem was. When he was done, he settled on the bed beside her.

Jennifer was an executive in a national recruitment agency. She travelled interstate a lot. Her hours and his were strange and she vowed they would never have children until they came to some sort of arrangement to settle down and share the responsibilities. Her view of his police work was jaundiced to say the least. How could anyone be happy investigating the horrible deaths of others?

"How's your day?" he asked.

"Okay," she said and added no more.

"What's up?"

"I think I've had enough," she replied.

"Enough of what?"

"You. Your job. Our marriage."

Kellogg was quiet and though he knew the strain his hours as a detective put on the marriage, he never considered their future was in doubt. He sincerely felt he was a good, reliable husband and she a good wife and a hard worker. He felt his job and hers were similar in the hours worked and the absences it caused between them.

"Do you love me?" he asked.

She was silent. He was shattered. They routinely told one another "I love you" when saying goodbye on the phone or leaving home. Most recently that was just this morning.

"What has happened to bring this on?"

She remained silent and could not look him in the eye. This was obviously serious.

"Tell me what has happened," he insisted.

She turned to him. "Your job has us apart so much. Look at the time now on a Saturday night. You are just getting home after working all day. Your work depresses you and there is usually no conversation. What do we have in common?"

"Your work has you away a lot too," he said.

"Yes. But it makes no difference to you. I am living with a boring policeman who investigates murders night and day. I hate what you do, and I don't want to talk about it. We do nothing as a couple that brings us together. These past two years we have grown apart."

He agreed with her, but she was the woman he loved and came home to. She was the stable one, the foundation for their marriage. He just couldn't imagine life without her.

"Why now? Why are you telling me this now? What has happened?"

"Last week the directors of my firm sounded me out to head up the Perth office. It is a promotion with some big money."

For Baz Kellogg the fact that she had always earned way more than his policeman's salary was a bonus. He wasn't ever jealous and just enjoyed the fact that they lived well on their combined income.

"Well, that's a real 'feather in your cap'… well done. Congratulations. And it's right we are talking about it now," he said. "So, let's weigh up the situation. Perhaps it is worth my while to transfer to the Western Australian police force."

"I accepted the position in writing today by email. I am going there alone at least for a time to give you and me a break. We need to sort out what this marriage is about, and I don't want you to come with me."

Baz Kellogg was devastated. He went to bed in the spare room. He didn't sleep much at all.

CHAPTER FOURTEEN

DC Dave Wells received a telephone call from a Mr Greenaway in response to the note Sam and he had left under his door when they called. He lived just a few doors away from the house where the mother had seen a cycle collide with a man.

"I'm sorry... I have just read your note. I have been away from home for a few days. How can I help you?" he asked.

"We are investigating an incident where a cyclist crashed into a pedestrian just across the road from your place. I wonder if you know anything... it was after 11 pm Wednesday night? Were you home then?"

"Yes. I was away for just Thursday and Friday nights. But at that hour on Wednesday, I would have been fast asleep."

"We've been asking all the people we can speak with in your street if they know of anyone with a personal security camera at their house?"

"I have a camera out front," he said.

Dave Wells went to see Mr Greenaway. He was happy to replay the relevant security footage. It was poor quality black and white and with badly focussed vision. His camera was at least 20 metres away from the action but showed the cyclist running into a pedestrian and knocking him over.

Wells asked to keep the CCTV footage. He took it straight back to Georgie.

CHAPTER FIFTEEN

Everyone in the team assembled early Sunday morning to review the case and share information. Georgie asked an assistant to lay out croissants, doughnuts, tea, and coffee in the HQ squad room.

In her research, Georgie had found that Dr Grace had no record with the police files. He had a life insurance policy for $750,000 and the sole beneficiary was his wife, Anne. The calls to and from his phone were very few. He seemed unsociable as there was little contact with anyone. Mostly he would call his wife, probably to say he was on the way home. There were about ten calls in the last month received from an untraceable number. Five of them were in the four days before he died.

Georgie had copied the vision from Mr Greenaway's somewhat primitive security camera and enhanced it as best she could. The team all watched the footage of the cyclist hitting the man on the street. From the improved vision Lazelle was satisfied the pedestrian was Dr Grace. There was no way to identify the raincoat-clad and helmeted cyclist.

"I feel it is safe to assume that this incident was the moment when Dr Grace sustained the injury," said Lazelle. "Could it have been an accident? I guess that's the first question."

Wells spoke. "We searched the exact spot where he fell. It occurred to us that there may have been a spike in the road or gutter. We looked for a loose wire in the fence nearby. We found nothing."

"If he fell on a spike, he would have bent it," Sam added. "It would have been painful. He would know he had been wounded and immediately gone back to hospital."

Lazelle thought for a moment. "Let's just think about the vision. The cyclist hit Dr Grace, then let the bike fall, but was extremely agile in landing on his feet and then bending over quickly, apparently to see if he was okay. Run the vision again Georgie. Zoom in if you can and slow it down for us to try and see what the cyclist did in those split seconds."

They ran the vision in close and half speed… it was not a very good picture, out of focus, but nevertheless provided further insight. You could see the bike was a standard road version with flat handlebars, a common model on the streets.

"There," said Lazelle. "The victim is knocked backwards and slightly onto his right side. The cyclist lets his bike slide away, lands confidently, then lunges forward apparently to help. Watch his right arm. Run it again Georgie."

As the vision is repeated Lazelle continued his commentary. "His right arm is moving quickly and ends up almost placed on the left side of Dr Grace's chest. There's no way he's trying to pick him up just then. The vision's not good enough to see a weapon but…" his voice faded.

"Now he helps him up to his feet," Lazelle said, "and they part with apparently some cordiality."

"It looks like they know one another," Georgie exclaimed. "Look at the acknowledgment after the incident. You don't deal with a stranger who has just knocked you down with that sort of familiarity."

"I am not sure we can make that assumption," said Lazelle. "It could be the rider apologising and Dr Grace forgiving the accident. It might just be cordiality. In any event with the helmet on and the raincoat hiding the body shape, I don't think the cyclist could be identified by the victim. And the whole encounter takes less than a minute."

They ran the vision again, up close, and slowly.

"Jesus," said Kellogg. "We've just witnessed a murder. That was the stabbing right there." The rest of the team murmured their assent.

Mid-afternoon Sunday, newspaper reporters and TV journalists with their camera crews were assembled at Victoria Police Headquarters in the media room. Detective Superintendent Pizzey and DI Lazelle fronted the gathering. They had decided that since the doctor's murder would soon become public knowledge it would be better to make the announcement themselves on a Sunday where it might attract less media coverage.

"Thank you all for being here," Pizzey said. "You are aware of a man being found dead on the last train to Hurstbridge, Wednesday night. We provided you all with CCTV footage from the train where a robbery occurred, and your coverage led us to find the youths involved and a witness whom we have interviewed. The victim was Dr Francis Grace. He was an anaesthetist at St. Barts hospital. That night he was involved in a late-night emergency surgery. I would like to hand you over to Detective Inspector Lazelle who is leading the investigation."

There was a murmuring amongst the gathering. Lazelle hated this part of the job. It didn't happen often, and he was a man who preferred to say very little. Nevertheless, this case was going to attract attention and Pizzey knew that Lazelle could find exactly the right words to say.

"Ladies and gentlemen. Again, thanks for your help so far. It is very early days in this investigation." He paused. "Dr Grace was murdered. The attack did not happen on the train. It happened somewhere between the hospital and North Richmond station before he boarded the train. The youths you have already seen on Metro CCTV robbed him but had nothing to do with his death. They took advantage of the unconscious man.

"We are asking anyone with information about Dr Grace's movements after surgery at St Barts hospital 10:15 pm last Wednesday night, and before he boarded the train at North Richmond station 11:17 pm, to contact the police hotline." He ended his announcement there.

"How was he killed?" asked a reporter.

"He was stabbed," Lazelle answered. "I can't say more than that."

"Why didn't he seek help?" asked another. "He was so close to the hospital."

"We believe he didn't know he was stabbed. The weapon was very thin and made a small wound."

There was a multitude of simultaneous questions that merged into a cacophony of indistinguishable sounds. "Please… one at a time," said Lazelle.

"If he was killed and the motive was not robbery, then is this a premeditated murder?" asked the TV journalist.

"It is early days. Thank you for your attendance and I urge anyone who knows anything about this matter to call us." With that Lazelle walked from the room. Pizzey thanked them and followed his detective out.

Much to Lazelle's dismay the news of the doctor's killing was flashed all over the TV, newspapers, and social media for the Sunday afternoon and evening. It was instantly a high-profile story and made headlines. The theme was about a stabbing that caused Dr Grace to die and that he was found on the train at the end of the line in Hurstbridge. The headlines read, "Doctor doesn't know he is dying", and "End of the line for the doctor" and, similar words. Not uncommonly the media took liberties with the known facts to create a sensation.

There was no mention of a cycle accident. Lazelle had not said anything about that. He wanted that information to remain hidden for the time being.

CHAPTER SIXTEEN

Lazelle and Kellogg went straight to the Van der Merwe's home. Unannounced, they knocked on the door, waited then knocked again. Emmie Van der Merwe answered. Recognising Lazelle from their previous encounter, she seemed surprised that he was there.

"How can I help you now?" she asked.

"Please may I come in?"

She showed the detectives into their elegant lounge room and signalled for them to be seated. She was in track pants and a sweater, no make-up. She still looked gorgeous he thought. "How can I help?" she asked.

"I have a few more questions based on further information that we have received. Did you ever meet Dr Grace?"

She thought for a moment never looking away.

"I saw him from time to time at the hospital Christmas lunch or some other event. I can recall at least having met most of my husband's theatre team at one time or another."

"Did he ever come here for dinner between finishing a surgery with your husband and having to go back to the hospital for a meeting?"

"Not that I know of."

"That would be about six months ago," the detective suggested.

She thought for a few moments. "Perhaps it was when I was out. I often arrange to have drinks and dinner with friends in the city. My husband works all hours, so I enjoy a social life without him. He might have helped Dr Grace out by ordering pizza and letting him come here during a break at the hospital. It is not very far from here as you know."

"Where is your husband now?"

"He took Colleen shopping in the city. They went only an hour ago and intend to have lunch there as well."

"Colleen is your daughter. She opened the door to us before."

"That's right. She is my daughter."

"When you say my daughter, is your husband the father?" he asked.

"No. She is a daughter by another man when I was young. We never stayed together. I married Johannes after we had our son Hansie who is thirteen now. When we got together my husband inherited a 6-year-old stepdaughter. They have always been close. He is the only father she has ever known."

"Is your daughter studying?"

"Yes. She is in her second year at the University of Melbourne doing a Media and Communications degree."

Lazelle decided to back off and end the conversation. "Please ask your husband to call me when he returns. My number is here." He handed her his card.

In the late afternoon, Van der Merwe telephoned.

"What do you want?" he abruptly asked.

"I would like to ask you a few more questions about Dr Grace. Firstly, when did you leave the hospital that night after surgery and how did you go home?"

"It was an emergency surgery so we didn't know we would be late. I usually walk to the hospital from home by day… if I had known I would be late I would have driven and parked the car there. That night I walked home."

"Where did you exit the hospital?"

"Out the front door I suppose."

"What do you mean you suppose?"

"Well, I may have gone down to the garage believing I had left my car there. It was a long night, I was tired, very tired after such concentration in surgery, and I might have done that."

"Which is it? Front door or garage?"

The surgeon was getting angry.

"Front door then," he snapped.

'Did Dr Grace ever come to dinner at your place after surgery and before a meeting back at the hospital?"

"I don't recall any such time."

"Are you sure because Mrs Grace thinks he did so about six months ago. Your wife thinks it must have been when she was out with her friends."

"As I said, I can't remember any such meeting at my house. We were not close. Colleagues. Professional. That's all."

"I am going to need to speak with you and your family again face to face."

"That's absurd man. You had better get your priorities straight. I'm done with talking to you." Then the surgeon abruptly ended the call.

Since her announcement she would go to Perth, Baz Kellogg and his wife Jennifer remained isolated in their own different worlds. She went out in the morning to have brunch with some friends. He was at work with Lazelle, quiet, and desperately unhappy.

They both arrived home late afternoon, and he offered to take her out for a meal, but she declined.

"When does this move take place?" he asked.

"In three weeks officially, but I think given the tension that I have caused between us I will take leave and go to Perth within the week. There will be things to do, find a flat, set up new contacts and so forth."

"Does this mean a divorce? Because we have financial matters to consider here with this house."

"For the moment let's see this as a separation to get our heads in the right place. I'll pay the same share of the mortgage and we will continue as it is."

Baz reached out and tried to hold her, but she firmly pushed him away. There was not going to be any further intimacy.

"It might not mean much to you now," he said, "but I love you and want to be with you. If you give me the chance I will change."

Baz Kellogg never asked if there was someone else in his wife's life because he never considered that as a possibility – and yet, he was a detective.

CHAPTER SEVENTEEN

At the team meeting, very early on Monday morning, everyone reported on their activities to date. In summary, they heard that Kellogg and Reed had interviewed all members of the surgical team except the surgical registrar. They found that tension existed between Van der Merwe and Grace. The Charge Nurse's recounting of the surgeon's comment about "quiet ones doing the most harm" established for all the detectives that something was wrong.

Georgie had no luck positively identifying Van der Merwe leaving the hospital that night. Even at that late hour many people were coming and going in different attire and often at angles that on the CCTV obscured their faces. She had enhanced the partial face of the cyclist from the security camera. With the helmet on it was hard to make much of it. But what seemed obvious was that under the raincoat the assailant was wearing a full-body Lycra suit. Glimpses of Lycra could be seen on the assailant's neck, face, lower legs, and wrists. The raincoat obscured any shape to the image, so it was impossible to say if the assailant was male or female.

In the parking garage there was nothing much to report. They had probably less than thirty names of staff that regularly used bicycles, and Lazelle urged the four uniformed police to reorganise shifts for a few more days and then quit when the duplications overwhelmed any new information. The bicycles parked in the hospital garage had all been carefully inspected for damage consistent with falling. No such damage had been found.

Starting that day, DC's Sam Long and Dave Wells were going to provide surveillance of Anne Grace on weekdays during school hours.

Lazelle recounted his meeting with Emmie Van der Merwe and the subsequent hostile phone call with the surgeon, and asked Georgie to check records both in Australia and in South Africa on both the husband and wife. He had decided that he and Kellogg would visit the family again this evening when they might all be home. He asked Kellogg to make the arrangement.

Meanwhile Lazelle had Georgie run the Greenaway CCTV footage of the stabbing again. They all watched it repeatedly at real time and slow speeds.

"What interests me most of all is the agility of the cyclist making a controlled dropping of the bike, landing deliberately on his feet, and then bending down to stab the victim, in almost the one fluent motion," said Lazelle. "And it all lasts no more than three or four seconds. This murderer is fit and agile."

He continued. "Say, Van der Merwe is a person of interest, is that him on the bike? At first sight he is fit enough but then again that fluency of movement. Could he do that after standing in a theatre operating for six hours? I think the assailant is a very experienced cyclist to be able to do that."

He had Georgie run the CCTV footage she had gathered of the half-hour from 11 pm at the front doors of the hospital. Lazelle studied it closely, sometimes backing up to re-run certain images. Of the many people leaving the hospital there were three clearly male figures of the same build as Van der Merwe that could not be positively identified.

Their clothing was nondescript. He asked for still shots of the three individuals.

When the meeting was over Lazelle pulled Kellogg aside to speak with him privately.

"What's up?" he asked his Sergeant. "Talk to me. I need you in good form and right now you are not doing so well."

"Sorry. There's nothing to tell right now. I'm okay," Kellogg lied.

CHAPTER EIGHTEEN

The pool cleaning guy pulled up outside Anne Grace's plush Eaglemont home at 10:30 am. Sam Long and Dave Wells, in an unmarked car, were instantly on duty. This was far preferable to the boredom of watching nothing at all.

He was young and handsome, mediterranean, dark, and muscular. Sam guessed he was mid-twenties. The guy gathered a carry tray of chemicals, cleaning agents and a few poles and brushes and entered the front driveway.

Wells stayed in the car while Sam Long went to see what she could. They had observed Anne Grace return from school 'drop off' and they knew she was in the house. Sam had to be careful not to be seen.

The young man went around the side to the pool in the back yard. He seemed to get right on with the job. Sam found a place where she could observe the pool area from the side of the house and out of sight from any window.

After twenty minutes, Mrs Grace came out with a coffee for the pool guy. They greeted one another and sat on a bench poolside talking. Sam could not hear what was said. After a while she took the empty mug from the young man and went inside. He returned to the pool cleaning. When he had finished, only an hour after arriving, he packed up his equipment and assembled it all by the pool bench. Then he went inside the house.

That's all Sam Long could see. She went back to the car and waited. Another hour later the pool guy brought his equipment out to the van and drove away. Wells had already noted the name of the pool cleaning company and phone number displayed on the van. He telephoned straight away and introduced himself. Then he asked for the name of the young man who serviced the pool at the Grace home in Eaglemont. The details were provided at once. They arranged with the company to make the cleaner available for interview that afternoon at the company offices.

DCs Long and Wells met the young man as arranged after school hours. Wells made the introductions and Sam took the lead.

"Your name is Donald Grimaldi?"

"Yes."

"How old are you?"

"Twenty-five."

"You service the pool at Mrs Grace's house in Eaglemont?"

"Yes."

"How long have you been doing that?"

"The company has had the contract for some time. I have been with the company for two-and -a-half years and have only been on the Grace's job for six weeks," he answered.

"Are you aware that in the last few days Dr Grace had been murdered?"

"Yes. It is awful."

"Mrs Grace must be devastated. I hear you were there today. How was she?"

"Oh, she is very upset. I just cleaned her pool, and she usually gives me coffee and I offered my sympathy."

"How did you hear the news of Dr Grace's death?"

"She told me today. She sat and talked with me and was upset."

"How long were you at her place?"

"About an hour."

Sam Long was weighing up what to say next… if she told him she knew what happened this morning that would expose their surveillance. Too soon she thought.

"Thank you for your time."

Sam called Georgie and asked her to find out whatever was on the record about Donald Grimaldi.

CHAPTER NINETEEN

Kellogg telephoned Emmie Van der Merwe. He explained to her that there were still matters they needed to follow up and so he and DI Lazelle would like to speak with their whole family together. She was reluctant, as quite obviously she had heard from her husband about the awkward phone call with Lazelle the day before. However, she agreed for the detectives to come to their home early that evening.

They sat down with the Van der Merwe family at the appointed hour.

"This had better be the last of it," snapped the surgeon. "This is bordering on police harassment."

Hansie the son was there, a strapping good-looking boy clearly in an advanced stage of puberty even at thirteen years of age. He was well built and muscular. He said in Afrikaans, "Moet ek hier wees?" His father immediately translated the question, "Does the boy have to be here?"

Lazelle observed the small gathering. The wife Emmie sat on a sofa next to her husband. She was trying her best to be helpful and seemed to be embarrassed by her husband's hostility. The son stood behind his parents waiting to be given permission to leave the room. The girl,

Colleen, sat in a single lounge chair to his right and was staring at her fingernails. All her body language said she did not want to be there. Lazelle and Kellogg were in the chairs opposite the sofa. They were seated around a beautiful rectangular rosewood coffee table.

"Your son can go," said Lazelle. "I'll do my best Doctor to make this as easy for you as I can. I cannot promise this is the end of our discussions. Remember this is an ongoing murder enquiry and I have every right to speak with those involved until I have the truth and we have found the guilty party."

"It's Mister," snapped the surgeon. "As a member of the Royal Australian College of Surgeons we lose the title Doctor and become elevated in the medical profession as Mister."

Lazelle never understood how the lofty promotion of top surgeons caused them to be addressed the same as any man on the street. 'Hand-me-down' British nonsense he reasoned.

"My apologies Mr Van der Merwe." He emphasised the 'Mister'.

The surgeon grunted but said no more.

"I have every reason to believe that Dr Grace was here for a makeshift dinner between surgery and another meeting at the hospital some six months ago. I believe something happened. Did Dr Grace come here as we have been led to believe?"

The surgeon blustered and took over the answer. "He might have, but if so, it was just the once and it was a favour to him because we live close by, and he had a meeting soon after at the hospital."

Lazelle looked at the wife. "I told you I was probably out with my friends. I have never seen Dr Grace in this house," she said.

The girl started to cry and ran out of the room. The wife immediately followed her.

"Now look what you've done," shouted the surgeon. Lazelle raised both hands to gesture calmly that this was necessary. Then he folded his arms. "We'll wait until they return."

There was an awkward silence for at least fifteen minutes until they came back.

"Colleen why are you so upset?" asked Lazelle.

She began to sob again. "I don't know why. I feel this is all wrong. And Josh is upset... that upsets us all."

Lazelle looked at the mother as if to ask the question that was immediately answered by Emmie gesturing towards her daughter. "She calls him 'Josh' and has done so ever since she accepted him as her stepdad thirteen years ago."

"Back to the question, Sir, why was there tension between you and Dr Grace? Why are others mentioning your remark about 'passion' to Dr Grace during the surgery? Why tell the Charge Nurse on one occasion that 'it's the quiet ones with closed minds that can do the most harm'?" Whereupon Colleen burst into tears again and quickly left the room.

The surgeon was now very angry. His voice was raised as he exclaimed, "this is a nonsense. What right do you have to enter my home and upset my family like this?"

"Sir. We have the right to do everything we can to find the person who killed Dr Grace. And now, we are talking with you and your family about your relationships with him."

"There was no relationship," snapped Van der Merwe. "And what you are talking about is just chatter."

More quickly this time, Emmie and Colleen re-entered the room. Deciding there was nothing to be gained by continuing the investigation this way, Lazelle rose from his seat and firmly addressed Johannes, Emmie, and Colleen Van der Merwe. "I am trying to do this as gently as I can. That's why we have come to your house so that you can be comfortable in your own environment and helpful with honest answers.

"Something happened between you and Dr Grace. We know it from other information we have. This family is hiding something from me, and I will find out what it is. I will finish what I hoped we might do this evening. But now we will do it the formal way. I intend to bring all three of you into Homicide HQ for individual interviews, that will be videotaped and on the record. I will have a female detective with me when we speak with Colleen. That will happen tomorrow. Detective Sergeant Kellogg will make suitable arrangements with you."

They were all visibly horrified. The surgeon was now blustering and not making much sense in his protestations as he followed Lazelle and Kellogg out.

At home Lazelle heated a packaged lasagne in the microwave then liberally coated it with tomato sauce and let it stand to cool for a minute. He poured a Scotch single malt whisky, dribbled a few drops of soda into the glass and took a sip. A firm believer that you should never drown a good whisky, he knew a few drops of water or soda simply released a much bigger flavour in a burst of aromatic bliss from the peat, or grain from wherever the distillery was.

He settled in his favourite black armchair, set the recline at a slight angle and felt comfortable in the home he had shared so happily with his late wife. Amid a case where there appears to be such relationship problems, he thought about his own life. After a lonely, almost withdrawn childhood he was fortunate to meet his wife, Jane, in their early twenties. She was a quietly competent woman who had the knack of getting him to express himself a little more.

After two miscarriages, they had a son, Andrew. Both parents regretted they could not have more children and that Andrew would grow up without siblings. Robin Lazelle was a good Dad, Jane a wonderful Mum and the boy did well at school and university, then became a financial planner with a major Australian bank. He married

Lily, they moved into their own home and eventually she had his grandsons, Johnny, and Keith. They were well-off and comfortable.

Lazelle and Jane remained very close to Andrew especially after he left home. They had nearly eight years as 'empty nesters' together and moved from the family home and downsized to the unit he still occupied. They loved walks, going to the movies, even just taking an occasional trip for a day and of course their planned annual holiday, usually at the beach and often in Fiji. They made a point of taking a regular annual holiday because that was the only way for him to stop thinking about his current case load. Lazelle found himself doing simple but enjoyable things in the company of the woman he had married long ago.

In a merciful way, she had been fit and well until a few pains and cramps were diagnosed as uterine cancer, and it had spread without warning. Her illness was terminal and despite treatment she lived just another seven months. She had passed away nearly four years ago.

Losing her was devastating to him. To escape the pain, he applied himself even more attentively to the cases he was investigating. He worked longer hours and sometimes, avoided being home. His team were sensitive to his loneliness. They tried to be of comfort, and to an extent he wanted to show he was grateful. However, he remained uncommunicative unless he had something critical to say about the investigation. He lived within his own self. They all knew Lazelle was a 'one-off and very special' even if different. Everyone marvelled at his clinical mind and sharp analysis.

He began eating the lasagne, trying to address his sadness and put the case out of his mind.

CHAPTER TWENTY

At the Tuesday team meeting Lazelle gave instructions.

"Sam, I want you to come off the surveillance and start enquiring about Colleen at university. See if she has any close friends. Dave, recruit one of the uniformed guys to help you watch Anne Grace. Keep that up during school hours. Nothing will happen when the kids are home.

"We can stop monitoring the cyclists at the hospital car park. There are only three hospital employees who used their cycles late that Wednesday night. They all have plausible alibis, and none are in any way connected with this case.

Georgie informed the meeting about information from her searches. "I have heard back from the South African Police about the Van der Merwe's. There's nothing dramatic, no misdemeanours. However, there is on the record a complaint by Emmie Van der Merwe's mother."

"What is that?" Lazelle asked.

"She accused Johannes Van der Merwe of sexually assaulting their granddaughter Colleen when she was just ten."

"What happened?"

"The grandmother made the complaint based on something Colleen told her. The police followed up and he, his wife and Colleen all denied any such thing. The grandmother's complaint was discredited, and the police had nothing to go on. There was a massive fallout between the Van der Merwe family and Emmie's parents. That's when the family planned to leave for Australia, although red tape prevented that from happening until just two years ago.

"And there's something else. The pool cleaner Donald Grimaldi has a record with Victoria Police. He was heavily into a youth gang and was charged several times for robbery and violence. He did two years' gaol time and was released three years ago. He has been working with the pool company these past two-and-a-half years and not been in any trouble since.

"One other thing," Georgie paused for effect. She was not shy to dramatise her information. "Donald Grimaldi was a BMX champion as a teenager. Even won a Victorian title."

The meeting was silent… only the older man Reed asked the question. "What in the world is BMX?"

They all smiled. Georgie explained.

"BMX is a track cycle competition over rough terrain with obstacles and jumps. You must be a very good cyclist to handle a bike that way. They do demonstrations where they make high jumps and do head over heels, somersaults, and stuff… Grimaldi must be an expert cyclist," Georgie answered.

Lazelle was thoughtful. Kellogg spoke. "This gives us justification for further questioning of Grimaldi."

"Let's just hold off for the moment," said Lazelle. "I want the surveillance of Anne Grace to last long enough to rule out any other men who may have been in her life. And we need to talk with the grandmother in South Africa. Georgie, get me her contact details. I will telephone her."

Sam Long spent the Tuesday morning and early afternoon at Melbourne University. She did this alone as it suited the investigations for her to apparently blend in as one of the students. Using her police ID and citing the urgency of a murder investigation, she spoke with the Dean of the faculty who had no idea who Colleen Van der Merwe was. He arranged for Sam to speak with the main lecturers in the girl's course. Colleen was not attending that day. No doubt she was still upset.

The lecturers were able to identify two female students who seemed to spend some time with Colleen. One of the staff introduced Sam to the girls after a lecture that coincidentally was that afternoon. They were shocked to hear about the investigation. They had no idea Colleen was involved. She had not communicated with them.

Their names were Julie and Michelle. The three sat on a bench in one of the courtyards near the Student Union Building. Sam explained that she would take notes and keep a record of their conversation.

"What can you tell me about Colleen Van der Merwe?" she asked them.

Julie answered first. "Not a lot. We used to sit together at some of our common lectures. We would eat lunch out here most of the days when we were all here. That happened about twice a week. Today would have been one of those days. It was just university course chit-chat mainly."

Sam looked to the other girl for her reply.

"It is like Julie says," said Michelle. "Not much more to add. We were not friends socially. We never saw her at any student parties or on nights out. She was pretty much a loner."

"Did she ever explain why?" asked Sam.

Michelle answered. "They are Afrikaaner's from South Africa. Traditionally prim and proper people. Personally, I felt she was really controlled by her stepfather who is a high-end surgeon and seemed to have an undue influence over Colleen."

"What did she say to give you that impression?"

Julie spoke this time. "As all girls do, we would sometimes talk about boys. Both Michelle and I have boyfriends, but we used to tease Colleen about getting close to some of the hot guys here. Colleen is a stunning blonde and the boys have noticed her. She never was interested though. She said she was okay the way things were."

"What did she tell you about her stepfather?"

"Just that they were close. He spoilt her. He was good to her."

"What about her mother?" asked Sam.

"They didn't have a proper mother-daughter relationship. They couldn't talk. Colleen used to get quite animated complaining about her mother being vain, never growing up, trying to stay young and beautiful, trying to be her sister and not a mother. She partied, acted like she was twenty and was not at all the responsible wife and mother she should be. Colleen also said her grandmother raised her until her Mum married the stepdad."

"That's a lot of information for a shy and conservative girl to share."

"Yes," added Michelle. "And to be honest, that's about the only time she would speak out and get personal. Her mother was obviously way out of touch with Colleen."

Sam checked her notebook to ensure everything was written down and thanked the girls for their time.

CHAPTER TWENTY-ONE

DC Dave Wells and a uniformed constable, Ray Saunders, continued the surveillance of Anne Grace for the school hours.

Wells was surprised to see Donald Grimaldi ride up on a bicycle, go down the side of the house and through the pool area. He was not in the pool van and obviously not working. Wells immediately rang the pool company and asked about Grimaldi. They said he had called and told them he was taking the morning off for personal reasons. Wells phoned Lazelle.

"It is very likely they are both spooked by him being interviewed yesterday," said Lazelle. "Just watch what happens. I will come over and we'll make a surprise visit."

Lazelle was there in thirty minutes. He had Constable Saunders stay out front in case Grimaldi tried to run. With Wells, Lazelle rang the doorbell. There was no answer. He rang again. Still nothing. After more than a minute Anne Grace answered, dressed in a track suit. She was quite horrified to see the detectives. She stepped aside for them to enter. They sat in the lounge.

Lazelle began. "Are you alone?" he asked.

"Of course," she answered. "Why do you ask?"

With that the front doorbell rang again. She rose, went to answer and there was an audible gasp. Constable Saunders pushed past her with Grimaldi collared.

"Oh, please do come in," said Lazelle with a degree of sarcasm. "Well done, Constable." As he entered the room, Grimaldi recognised DC Dave Wells from their interview the day before and his face blanched. The police again. For someone who knew well the other side of the law, he had grave misgivings about his present position.

"I think we have some matters to clarify here," said Lazelle. "You, Mrs Grace, a grieving widow, your husband murdered only six days ago, are entertaining this young man here today. You have been under surveillance for some days, and we also know this man was here indoors with you for an hour yesterday.

"You, Mr Grimaldi, have taken this morning off work for personal reasons and here you are with Mrs Grace. So, this is your personal reason. I warn both of you, this is a murder investigation. I am going to interview you individually. Your answers had better be truthful or you will be charged with obstructing the investigation. And if of course you have anything to do with the death of Dr Grace there are grave consequences ahead."

There was an awkward silence while Lazelle paused and watched them both. Then he said, "Constable, take this man and sit in the car outside. Mr Grimaldi, when we have finished speaking with Mrs Grace we will come and talk to you."

The Constable, still with a hold on Grimaldi's collar, left the house. Lazelle motioned to Kellogg and Mrs Grace to sit back down.

"How do you explain him being here?" he asked her.

Anne Grace looked extremely uncomfortable. She wished she could vaporise before them and end up in some happier place. After a time, she signed to Lazelle. "Does this have to be on the record?"

Wells was taking notes and looked confused when Lazelle signed back. "Yes, it does. We must know what is happening here as part of our investigation." Then he spoke. "Please answer the question."

"Donald has been cleaning our pool for six weeks now and I suppose about a month ago I invited him inside. One thing led to another, and he was happy to oblige me. It hasn't been long, and he is not to blame. As you well know my husband and I have been remote from one another for many years and certainly as good as separated for the past six months."

Lazelle paused then said, "For the record and to assist the investigation I need to know, are you and Mr Grimaldi in a sexual relationship?"

She looked away and out the window. "Yes, we have been," she said.

"You are clearly not mourning the loss of your husband?"

"Of course, I mourn his loss. Maybe not in a deep sadness. His death does not serve me and our children well. His income, this lifestyle was what we enjoyed. We will miss that and there will be financial adjustments. I didn't want anything to change. I tolerated his lack of emotion and lack of intimacy, and only recently found some satisfaction in having Donald with me."

"Will this continue? Is it an emotional bond?"

"You mean is it a love affair?" she asked. "Don't be ridiculous. I am sure I speak for us both by saying it is purely physical. And it won't continue."

"Did you ever discuss your husband with Grimaldi?"

"No. All he really needed to know was that my husband was at work."

"You saw him yesterday. Why did he come back today?"

"Yesterday, when I told him, it was the first time he knew anything about my husband's murder. He was shocked. This morning, he rang me and said you had interviewed him and that he didn't want any trouble and needed to see me."

"And so today, what has happened between you?"

"Nothing like that. He was upset and wanted to end what we were doing. He told me that he had been in trouble before with the law and did not want to be involved with a police murder investigation."

Lazelle paused for a moment. "I have one last question. Are there any other men in your life? Is there anyone who might want to see your husband out of the way to be with you?"

Anne Grace seemed shocked. As if it wasn't embarrassing enough to be found with a young man such as Donald Grimaldi, now the detective was accusing her of being a loose woman. "No, No. No." she said loudly and with obvious disgust.

"Thank you for your honesty," said Lazelle.

With that the detectives left the house. Lazelle made a slight detour to the side driveway to take a close look at Grimaldi's bicycle. Though the vision of the assault on CCTV was poor, the bike involved was a common make with flat handlebars. Not much to go on, but Grimaldi's bike was the same. There were no marks or damage. However, as a competition cyclist he would have a BMX bike somewhere.

CHAPTER TWENTY-TWO

Back in the car, Wells and the Constable were in front and Lazelle sat alongside Grimaldi in the back seat.

"So, Donald, why are you here today?" asked Lazelle.

"I was shocked to be interviewed yesterday as part of a homicide investigation. I came here to talk with Anne about what had happened and to tell her I wanted out and that someone else would clean her pool in future. I intend to tell my employer about this. I am serious about going straight. I have a good job. I don't want any part of a murder enquiry.

"I like Anne. I have had my problems in the past. I will own up and say you will find I have been in gaol. Since my release my record is clean. My work is good. I am a reliable employee and have never been in any trouble."

"Did she ever talk about her husband with you?"

"Not really. I knew he was a doctor, and you could tell from the plush home they were well off. She is a nice woman, and I enjoyed her company."

"You were in a sexual relationship?"

"Yes... that's all. It has just been a very short time. No other feelings," said Grimaldi.

Lazelle paused a while and let the man wonder how much trouble he was really in.

"In a murder investigation we must consider all possibilities and rule out one by one every likely scenario. For example, one such possibility is that Mrs Grace had you murder her husband. Where were you on Wednesday night last week?" asked Lazelle.

Grimaldi started to shake and seemed to be on the verge of tears. "No, no... that's absurd. I had nothing to do with him... she never suggested any such thing."

"Calm down," said Lazelle more gently. "Just tell me where you were Wednesday night?"

"I was at home in the flat I share with two other guys. They were out drinking. I was meant to go with them, but I didn't feel up to it. I went to bed."

"You were a BMX cycle champion?" asked Lazelle.

"Yeah. As a teenager I rode in competitions and was sponsored by the bike company. Stopped about the age of nineteen. Before that I was high in the ratings and at age 17 won the state title."

"Do you still ride your BMX bike?"

"Not much. I have a road bike I use to get around. It's the one I rode here today."

Lazelle nodded. "Give your address and your flat mates' names and phone numbers to DC Wells and you can go."

Dave Wells phoned the two mates. It took several calls but eventually he spoke to them and arranged to interview each man face to face later that day. He met the first, a guy called Jimmy, at a coffee shop near their flat.

Wells explained the reason for the interview. "I'm from the Homicide squad, and we are investigating a murder. As part of our investigations, I need to know where Donald Grimaldi was on Wednesday night. He says he was at your flat and that you and your other mate were out drinking."

Jimmy had obviously been warned by Grimaldi that the police were going to interview him.

"Matty and I were out drinking in a bar in King Street from around 6:30 pm until maybe 10 pm."

"When did you get home?" asked Wells.

"I guess it was around 10:45 pm. We took an Uber home because we'd had a lot to drink."

"Was Donald home then?"

"I think so. We have separate bedrooms, and his door was closed. I know he didn't feel so good and went to bed early."

"Did he say anything to you about having an affair with an older woman... a client of his pool cleaning company?" asked the detective.

Jimmy laughed out loud. "Yeah. It was a bit of fun for Don. Good looking, he said... nice to be with her."

"Did he say anything more about her husband?"

"He knew she was married to a doctor and not happy. And I only found out yesterday when Don told me that the husband was murdered. That was after you guys spoke with him. He said you would talk to me. I can vouch for him. He had nothing to do with the crime. He is determined to go straight, and he won't be seeing that woman again."

"You and Matty left the bar and arrived home together?"

"Yeah, we were drunk... it was a long session. We didn't eat much and had way too many beers," Jimmy said.

"One last question. Donald was BMX champion. Does he have bicycles?"

"Yes two. There's a common road bike then there's the BMX one."

Wells interviewed the other young man, Matthew, at his workplace and his story was the same. He and Jimmy had been drinking at a King Street bar, a common night spot for the young twenties. The bar was one which stayed open until 2 am. By the sounds of it they were both well and truly intoxicated and gave up early and arrived home at 10:45 pm. They went to bed and were so 'dead to the world' that they could not possibly know if Grimaldi was asleep in his room. Nor would they have heard him if he was out and came home later.

DSC Reed joined DC Wells at Grimaldi's flat. Grimaldi was apprehensive as he let the detectives into the sparsely furnished sitting room. They sat on what could only be described as picnic chairs.

"We still need to verify you were in bed on the evening of Dr Grace's death. Your flatmates came home drunk but cannot positively say that you were in your room asleep."

"I told you," Grimaldi said. "I was in bed. I felt unwell."

"Your mates say your door was closed so they didn't see you."

"That's how I sleep… with the door closed. How else can I prove it?"

"Let us have your phone to establish your movements," said Wells.

"Sure. But I need it. How long is this going to take?"

"I'll make sure you have it back tomorrow," Wells assured him.

Reed asked to see the bicycles. The BMX one had flat handlebars and was well knocked about as you might expect of a trick cycle where there must have been many accidents at practice trying to perfect a stunt.

"We will need to examine that bike," said the policeman.

"Sure," said Grimaldi. "Take the bike. Do what you want. I have nothing to hide."

CHAPTER TWENTY-THREE

Early afternoon Emmie and Colleen Van der Merwe were brought into Homicide Headquarters in a police car. The surgeon was given a pass to consult patients and then he would be collected later by a squad car as well. Lazelle knew that the psychological effect of being 'picked up' by the police and formally interviewed would emphasise the gravity of their position and hopefully weaken their resistance.

It was no surprise that Van der Merwe had arranged for a senior solicitor from an eminent Melbourne law firm, Patterson & Partners, to arrive at HQ and sit with each of the family members during the interviews. The lawyer introduced himself as Geoff Wilson.

Lazelle deliberately chose to interview Colleen first and to leave the mother alone waiting in another room. He was joined by DC Long. Sam did the formal identification for the benefit of the recordings.

"This is Detective Constable Sam Long. I am accompanied by Detective Inspector Robin Lazelle, and we are interviewing Ms Colleen Van der Merwe in the matter of the homicide of Dr Francis Grace. Ms Van der Merwe is accompanied by her lawyer Mr Geoff Wilson of Patterson & Partners.

"May we call you Colleen?"

"Yes," the girl answered.

"Colleen, I am obliged to inform you that this is a formal police interview. It is being recorded and videotaped. What you say may become evidence in any subsequent court proceedings. You must tell the truth… any untruths will be seen as impeding these investigations and becomes a serious matter. I am obliged to tell you that you may decline to answer questions if you believe the answers will incriminate you."

Wilson answered for her. "She knows that."

Sam Long quickly responded, "Colleen, you must verbally acknowledge that you understand what I have just said. Your lawyer cannot answer for you."

Colleen said, "I understand what you have told me."

Lazelle took over. "Colleen. For the record, how old are you?

"Nineteen," she answered.

"And you are the daughter of Emmie Van der Merwe and stepdaughter of Johannes Van der Merwe?"

"Yes."

"How long has your mother been married to your stepdad?"

"They've been together about fourteen years. They married after Hansie was born thirteen years ago."

"Did you know Dr Francis Grace?"

The girl looked down and was silent for a while. Lazelle waited patiently. Silence in this situation was golden for the detectives and purgatory for the respondent. She looked at the lawyer who nodded she should answer.

"Yes," she said, surprising her lawyer.

"How so?" asked Lazelle.

"He came to the house with Josh after surgery about six months ago. I met him for the first time then, and we ordered pizza for us all. Dr Grace was with us for about two hours and then returned to the hospital for a meeting."

"Did anything out of the ordinary happen?"

"What do you mean?"

"We have been told that after that evening things between your stepdad and Dr Grace were tense. Did something happen that evening?"

The girl whispered something to the lawyer, and he nodded.

"So, what happened?" asked Lazelle.

"We all sat together eating the pizza. Josh and Hansie were there in the beginning. After about 30 minutes, Josh went to his study to work and Hansie went to his room. It was just me and Dr Grace left together. It was quite awkward. We had never met before. He was a much older guy, and at first, it was hard for me as a teenager to engage with him. As well, Dr Grace is a very shy and conservative man… he found it hard to make conversation. To be polite, and because Josh had been rather rude in walking away and leaving us stranded, I started to talk about myself and what I was doing at university.

"He recalled his experience at the same age and his feelings. It went well from there. We spent at least an hour together before he had to go back to the hospital. He was easy to talk to. In fact, he listened to me as I had rarely ever experienced before. He was talkative too. Surprisingly, things between us became very comfortable."

"What sorts of things did he tell you?" asked Lazelle.

"He compared his teenage experience at university in Oxford with mine here in Melbourne. Thirty years ago, Oxford University was ultra-conservative, and he told me how he became over-awed and introverted. He couldn't really talk to anyone. He had no close friends. There was no emotional support, so he battled on with his studies trying to feel better and often he felt worse. You know, I don't think he had ever said that to anyone before. He told me within an hour of us meeting."

"What did you tell him?"

"I shared some similar feelings, and he understood what I was going through. It was astonishing really."

Lazelle thought for a moment before his next question. "In the other meeting I have had with you and your parents at your home, the mention of Dr Grace's death has caused you to break down in tears and leave the room. I have the feeling now that you formed a close relationship with him. Did you contact or see him again after that evening?"

Again, the girl looked at her lawyer. "Answer the question," he said.

"Yes, from time to time. I could telephone him. If I didn't have university and if he was between operations we might meet in the park, sit on a bench with take-away coffee and sandwiches and talk. It was always very proper, and he was a kind man. I was also able to help him in some ways. He certainly helped me with some problems I had."

"Was the relationship between you ever romantic?"

"Oh no," the girl replied firmly. "It was just two people who had found someone to share feelings with. Almost like two people sitting on a plane together talking about personal things with someone they didn't know and who was not part of their close social circle and would never tell anyone to embarrass you."

"Do you have a boyfriend, a romantic interest?"

"No."

"Not ever... no boyfriend at school or university?"

"Maybe some silly flirting at school, but no."

Lazelle paused for a few moments looking directly at the girl as if to weigh up her honesty. "Did you use your own phone to call Dr Grace?"

"At first yes. But in the last month he bought a cheap 'burner phone' for me to use. It was an untraceable number. He said he didn't want me to call on my own phone and that things between him and Josh were becoming difficult. Also, he wanted me to be able to call him if it was urgent. He felt something might happen. He told me to call, not text. When he was killed, I was devastated. It was like he knew something, and that somehow, I might be responsible."

"If your relationship with Dr Grace was so platonic, why the need for an untraceable phone?"

"I think he felt it would not compromise him or myself with his family or mine. Nothing we spoke about can be traced."

"It seems very odd… not at all the usual way for a normal friendship to go," Lazelle said. "What were you hiding if it was not an affair?"

"Some of what I was talking with Dr Grace about was very intimate… not physically, but emotionally. I did not want my parents to know what I told him."

"I think what you were talking about is crucial to this investigation. What was it?" asked Lazelle.

She turned to her lawyer, "Can I claim those discussions as private and confidential?"

"Just decline to answer," the lawyer asserted. Then he instructed Lazelle, "Let's move on."

"Where is the burner phone now?" Lazelle knew that if they could lay hands on it there might be ways to find out more.

"When I heard of his death, I threw it into a public waste basket. It was just for me to call him and with him gone, that was over."

Lazelle was silent for a moment. He felt sure she was hiding something very important that would likely provide a motive for the demise of Dr Francis Grace.

"So, when your stepfather came back into the room that evening when Dr Grace was still there, what did he see? What upset him?"

"I really don't remember. Francis, sorry Dr Grace, was sitting next to me. I know I was in a sort of tearful mood, and he had from time to time put his hand on my shoulder to console me. Josh may have seen that and felt it was inappropriate."

"You called him Francis?" Sam Long asked.

"Not at the start, but he asked me to call him that later on."

Lazelle continued. "After Dr Grace left, what happened between you and your stepdad?"

"He was very angry. He asked what we had been talking about. I told him we were comparing our university experiences. He could see I was emotional. He asked if Dr Grace had acted inappropriately with me. I told him no."

"Did he know you kept seeing Dr Grace after that first meeting?"

"No."

"Did your mother know?"

"No."

"You kept your subsequent meetings with Dr Grace secret from them?"

"Yes."

"Let's assume your stepdad fell out with Dr Grace because he suspected he was acting inappropriately with you. Why did you continue to see the man?"

"Francis became very important to me. He helped me to feel better about myself. He was also comfortable with me. The relationship was like having a real caring father figure."

"Isn't your stepdad that father figure to you?"

"No."

"You don't trust your stepdad?"

"No."

"Why not?"

The girl took her time with the next answer choosing her words carefully. "He is all about his own needs and has no consideration for mine."

"What about your mother?" asked Lazelle. "Can't you confide in her?"

By now Colleen was in tears. Not the sort of emotional outburst that he had seen before. These were silent tears from deep within. "No. She's not interested in being my Mum. She wants to be my sister. She wants to stay glamorous and young. She resents growing older and has a multitude of problems of her own."

Lazelle put the three photographs of men leaving the hospital on the table. "Are any of these men your stepdad?" he asked.

She looked at the photos closely studying each one. "It is hard to say… the second one looks like it might be him. That jacket looks like his."

"One last question," added Lazelle. "Do you ride a bicycle?"

"We all do. We used to ride in the park together. That probably hasn't happened so much of late… not since I've been at Uni anyway."

"Who still rides now?"

"My Mum most of all. She has always been a cyclist even in South Africa. Hansie rides with his friends too."

"Where were you on Wednesday night?"

"At home. I went to bed early. Hansie was in his own room too."

"Was you mother home?"

"She was out some of the time. I don't really know. We keep to ourselves, in our own rooms," Colleen answered.

Lazelle summed up the interview with some final comments. "I feel that whatever you and Dr Grace were sharing is crucial to this investigation. We will need to find out what that is. Under advice from your lawyer, you have declined to go into the matter here today, but I must warn you that you will be obliged to answer such questions under oath in any legal proceedings. For the moment I will let it pass."

CHAPTER TWENTY-FOUR

DS Baz Kellogg formally introduced the interview with Emmie Van der Merwe and provided the obligatory cautions to her in the presence of her lawyer Geoff Wilson. She was on edge, having been kept waiting in an enclosed room while she knew her daughter was being interviewed. That was exactly the effect Lazelle had hoped for.

"You are Emmie Van der Merwe, wife of Johannes and mother of Colleen?"

"Yes," she replied.

"How old are you?"

"I am 37 years old. I had Colleen with another man when I was just eighteen. It was a just a fling. She never knew him."

"May I ask what your occupation is?"

"I don't work now. I used to be a paramedic in South Africa. That is how I met my husband."

Lazelle placed the three photos of men leaving the hospital on the table in front of her. "Can you identify any of these men as your husband?"

She looked closely at each photo. Picked up the second one, looked again, then placed it back before Lazelle. "That's him. Where is this?"

"They are photos of men leaving the hospital about the time your husband was going home from the late-night operation. Your husband said he walked home."

"He did walk home… it was a surprise he had to stay for emergency surgery, so he didn't have his car."

"Do you know of any reason why your husband had issues with Dr Francis Grace?"

"No."

"How well did you know Dr Grace?"

"Not well. We met a few times in the past two years at hospital staff celebrations… there have been consultant physicians' thank you dinners, then Christmas and the like. We have acknowledged one another on such occasions."

"Why do you think your daughter is so upset by Dr Grace's death?"

"I can't say. Maybe she felt for Josh losing such a valuable member of his surgical team."

"That really doesn't explain the tears and leaving the room at our previous meeting," said Lazelle. "It is one thing to feel for her stepdad. It is another thing to be distraught about the death of a man she supposedly didn't know. You went to console her on those occasions. What did she tell you?"

"Nothing. It was just all tears and teenage emotions." she replied.

Lazelle remained silent for a time leaving Emmie to consider her answers. She was being deceptive. Then abruptly he asked, "Did you know Colleen had a continuing relationship with Dr Grace that began when he came to your house about six months ago?"

She didn't answer. Rather than look surprised, she looked embarrassed and whispered to the lawyer who nodded in assent. Then she answered.

"I suspected something. Her attitude changed. But I didn't know for sure."

"Did you ask her?"

"I did but she said there was nothing to worry about."

"Why do you think she kept seeing Dr Grace?"

"I don't know." She stopped short, appeared to think about the question for a moment and added, "I really don't know."

"What is your marriage like? Are there any problems at home?"

"Our marriage is okay. My husband is almost always on the job. Since I have been in Australia, unlike South Africa, I have enjoyed the freedom of being safe everywhere and have developed some good friends to socialise with. I get out and about quite often."

"What about your son Hansie? Doesn't he need you to be around?"

"He's a young adolescent now. Quite independent. And most evenings Colleen is with him if I am out."

Lazelle continued. "May I ask if you, Mrs Van der Merwe, ride a bike?"

"Yes."

"Are you a regular rider... do you ride with a group?"

"No. I ride alone here in Melbourne We are near parklands and that is my daily routine. Hansie sometimes rides with me."

"Did you ride in South Africa?"

"Yes, I have been a cyclist for years but back there it was not safe to just ride anywhere. So much crime. Women were often raped in broad daylight. I would only ride in the protected neighbourhood and parklands near where I lived and under the watch of the estate's private security guards."

"Where were you on the night your husband worked late at around 11:00 pm?"

"At that hour on a Wednesday I was home. I would have gone to bed by then. I socialise mostly on Friday and weekends."

"Does your husband ever ride his bike to work?"

"No. He walks if his hours are daytime. He drives if the day ends late."

"How about Colleen?"

"She walks to the tram and goes to university. Sometimes she might ride with me in the park, but not much."

"And Hansie?"

"He uses his bike quite a lot. It is the only transport for a thirteen-year-old to go meet his friends."

And with that Kellogg formally ended the interview.

CHAPTER TWENTY-FIVE

Later that day Johannes Van der Merwe was brought into the Homicide HQ by police car. Lazelle insisted this happen to emphasise the importance of proceedings and to intimidate the surgeon. This was not going to be an occasion where the man could attempt to take control.

Kellogg did the introductions. The lawyer Wilson was again present to protect the interests of his client.

"What were your issues with Dr Grace?" asked Lazelle.

"We were colleagues in the operating theatre. We were a good team. Everyone would say so if you care to ask them."

"Why is your stepdaughter so upset about his death?"

"She is a teenager with issues. I guess it was just an upset that happened to our family… something she thought upset me especially. We are close."

"Do you now recall having Dr Grace in your home for pizza before he had to go back to the hospital for a meeting?"

"I think so. It was not a moment of any significance."

"On that evening you went to your study and left Colleen and Dr Grace alone for more than an hour. She has told us so. They talked at length and seemed to establish a close relationship that continued until his death. That is why she is so upset."

"What do you mean?" The surgeon looked mildly surprised.

"They continued to see one another. She thought well of him. She is very upset that he was murdered. That's what I mean," Lazelle said.

"I know nothing about that." The surgeon folded his arms defiantly.

"Did your wife ever speak to you about Colleen having further dealings with Dr Grace?"

"No."

"Do you ride your bike?"

"Maybe on rare occasions with my wife in the park. But not much."

"Your wife and Hansie use their bicycles the most then?"

"Yes."

Lazelle placed the photos of the three men leaving the hospital before the surgeon. "Can you identify yourself leaving the hospital?" he asked.

Without hesitation Van der Merwe picked up the second photo and said, "that's me."

Lazelle addressed the surgeon directly. "I have no doubt you and your family will have many things to talk about after this. We have it on record that Colleen continued meeting and calling Dr Grace, whether purely platonic for conversation or possibly an affair. They became close to one another, and his death is a painful loss to her. There will be more questions in future. Every member in your family is a person of interest."

Van der Merwe made no reply and after a moment of silence Kellogg declared the interview over. Apart from opening and closing the interview, he had said nothing and seemed lost in his own thoughts.

When Lazelle and Kellogg were alone, Lazelle asked sensitively, "How are things? And are you okay?"

"Yes of course," Kellogg pushed back. "Just some problems with my wife."

"If you want to talk, I'm here for you. I know I'm not the greatest communicator in the world, but you're an important colleague and I need you to be switched on."

"Thanks. I'm okay."

After a short break to get his thoughts together, Kellogg went to the hospital to meet Dr Anton Delaney, the surgical registrar assisting in the late evening surgery. Delaney was around thirty years old and looked apprehensive. He was a fit man, blonde and blue-eyed.

"Thanks for your time," Baz Kellogg began. "You have no doubt heard about Dr Grace's untimely passing. What did you know about him?"

"I guess everything you've already been told. He was a good anaesthetist and a quiet, reserved man."

"On the night of the late surgery, I have been told that something was said by Mr Van der Merwe to Dr Grace after you mentioned your girlfriend running hot and cold?"

Delaney blanched. "I can't really remember that happening. There's always banter during surgery, especially the ones that take several hours."

"Apparently, Van der Merwe turned to Dr Grace after you made whatever the remark was and said something like 'What do think about passion Frankie?' Everyone heard it and the others have mentioned it as a memorable moment."

"I know they had issues," said Delaney. "Their relationship had become very strained especially in recent months. I don't attend all their surgeries and only assist on a rostered basis. I assist with other surgeries as well. It is all part of my final training to be admitted to the Royal Australian College of Surgeons."

"May I ask how you went home that evening?"

"I have a car in the car park."

"Are you married or was the remark about a girlfriend?"

"I am not married and enjoy being single. My girlfriends change and I have no steady relationship."

CHAPTER TWENTY-SIX

As Lazelle left the Homicide HQ, Anthony Rowen, a long-time crime reporter from the Herald, Melbourne's highest circulating newspaper, intercepted the well-known detective. This reporter had covered many cases, had written books about major crime stories, and was often better connected to the police than Lazelle himself. He had informants everywhere and the leaks to him were proliferous.

"So, Lazelle." They were not on first name terms, and much to Lazelle's displeasure the journalist just called him by his surname without any dignified title. The detective had no time for the man and detested his work, though he had to admire Rowan's tenacity and what he was able to uncover. He had often featured in media interviews and had broken some good stories in his career.

"What's up?" asked the reporter.

"What do you mean 'what's up'?"

"Word is out that you have today interviewed the Van der Merwe surgeon and his wife and daughter. Why?"

'Word is out' There he goes again thought the detective. What word? Whose word? Where's the leak? He doubted his own people would speak with the man.

"It is all part of an ongoing investigation. Mr Van der Merwe was the lead surgeon in an operation that went late into the Wednesday night just before Dr Grace was killed."

"I get why you are talking to him. But the wife and daughter? Why?"

"It is all part of understanding the surgical team, Dr Grace and his movements." replied Lazelle.

"Lazelle… c'mon?" The journalist was aware he was being 'snowed'. "The wife and daughter? They have nothing to do with the surgical team."

"The investigation is in its early days. We need to know what the victim has been doing, why he was where he was, what happened and who he knows."

"So, how did he know the wife and daughter?"

"No comment. Good evening, Mr Rowan."

Lazelle went home. He needed a time-out to think. The case was becoming more complicated by the minute. After a shower, a chicken Caesar salad, and a glass of wine, he settled in his favourite chair with a single malt Scotch whisky and a dash of water. A nightcap he might say. A 'digestif' as the French would have it. He stared into space, cleared his mind, and thought. In every case he always tried to take a personal time-out just to think about what was known and put aside any guesswork or hunches. What are the facts? What are the things we know for sure?

He thought to himself: "Francis Grace was found on a train very late Wednesday night and died from a stab wound in the small hours of last Thursday morning. We found the kids that robbed him and retrieved his belongings. We identified him as an attending anaesthetist at St. Barts Hospital in North Richmond. He had been on duty with the surgeon Van der Merwe in an emergency operation until late night Wednesday.

"Very poor-quality video evidence shows the murder was committed by a cyclist in the back streets when the victim was walking from the hospital to catch a train home. We know it happened around 11:09 pm. The cyclist was wearing a helmet, and a raincoat that covered three-quarters of a full-body Lycra clad person. The figure was of medium height, with what seemed an athletic physique and could have been male or female.

"There was bad blood between the surgeon and the victim. The snide comment about 'passion' made by Van der Merwe during the surgery certainly suggests a source of aggravation between the two. It most likely has to do with a secret relationship, platonic or otherwise, between Francis Grace and the Van der Merwe daughter, Colleen. Perhaps the surgeon saw something between them at his home about six months ago. The derogatory comment aimed at Grace during surgery about 'passion' suggests so. The mother suspects something as well.

"There was a continuing relationship between Dr Grace and Colleen, and their liaison was so secret that he provided her with a burner phone so she could contact him without trace. She called him several times in the last few days. She discarded the phone after his death. We have no idea what they were doing together. She claims he was a father figure helping her with emotional issues. Colleen has no boyfriend and, no love interest, so we must consider she may have become besotted with and even intimate with the victim. She denies that firmly. However, they were so close that his death has caused her significant grief.

"Maybe the Van der Merwe's had reasons to end a perceived affair between Dr Grace and their daughter. There is certainly something very wrong in that family and we don't know what it is. Only Colleen seems likely to tell us.

"The collection of data in the parking garage has done nothing to lead us to any hospital rider being a suspect. Photos of people leaving the front door of the hospital at that hour seem to suggest that the surgeon is one of them and that he did walk home after the operation. His whole family have independently identified the same CCTV photo as him. He could not have been in the back streets to commit the crime. That rules him out as the assailant.

"Francis Grace was not well liked and had no friends. He was considered cold and unapproachable by his colleagues, his wife and his in-laws."

Lazelle had every sympathy for a man who kept to himself, did not talk much and was not comfortable socialising. That was his own experience. From his dysfunctional family beginnings, he was withdrawn as a child. As an adult he had preferred to stay away from social gatherings and his interaction with others was mainly professional. He was not going to condemn the man for feeling that way.

Lazelle continued his silent analysis: "Sonia Baker has suggested there was no love lost between husband and wife. She even hinted that her friend was having a casual affair... albeit jokingly and maybe not for real, Anne Grace described herself as a 'cougar'.

"Sam Long witnessed the young pool guy, Donald Grimaldi, cleaning the Grace's pool and then spending an hour indoors with Mrs Grace. We caught them out the next day. She has admitted they were in a sexual relationship. We know Grimaldi was and probably still is an expert cyclist. Did Anne Grace convince him to murder her husband for the insurance money? Though given her multi-million-dollar home, a specialist doctor's high income, a life insurance payout of $750,000 was very modest in such circumstances, and no real incentive to see her husband dead.

"Forensics have carefully gone over Grimaldi's BMX bike. They have looked at the scene of the attack to establish the asphalt and dirt nearby to compare with any traces of similar materials on the cycle. Despite the many scratches, dents, marks and dirt on the BMX bike, nothing from the crime scene can be identified exclusively.

"Grimaldi's phone records have been examined by Georgie. The phone hadn't moved from his flat the night in question. Whilst that is not a firm alibi... the phone could have been left at home while he was out... for the moment, it appears that Grimaldi is telling the truth.

"Did the victim know his killer? We can see an almost apologetic and cordial exchange after the so-called accident. The killer is fit and a competent bike rider. The controlled fall and stabbing in a continuous few seconds' movement are not easily done. The only regular cyclists we know about are Donald Grimaldi, Emmie Van der Merwe and her son, Hansie."

These thoughts summed up perfectly what was already evident.

Lazelle finished his whisky and put his glass on the kitchen bench. He looked through the window to see it was raining again. He turned off the lights and sat for a little while longer in his chair trying to become calm and to put the case out of his mind. He felt tired and quite often a little out of breath. He swore this case was making him unwell. All in the mind of course. After a while he went to bed. He slept surprisingly well.

CHAPTER TWENTY-SEVEN

The very next morning, with a search warrant to access the Van der Merwe home, DCs Long and Wells, accompanied by uniformed police and a forensic lab specialist, moved through the house room by room, finding nothing of any real interest. They took away all laptops, and the one-piece black Lycra riding suit Emmie owned. There was no sign of a raincoat.

Then they took all four bicycles and helmets from the garage. Each was labelled as to who owned which bike and taken to forensics. The Lycra suit also went to forensics with a request to look for any bloodstains.

The laptops were given to Georgie for analysis. She determined within a few hours there was nothing of interest on the computers.

With help from Georgie, who had obviously impressed someone in the Cape Town police, Lazelle quickly had the telephone number for Emmie Van der Merwe's parents. They were Mr and Mrs De Villiers. Allowing for the time difference, he rang late afternoon, so early morning in South Africa. Courtesy of the local police, Mrs De Villiers had received notice of the call and some background to the investigation of the murder of her estranged son-in-law's colleague.

"Hello Mrs De Villiers. Thank you for taking my call. My name is Detective Inspector Robin Lazelle from the Victoria Police in Australia. I am investigating the murder of Dr Grace who was the anaesthetist in operations conducted by your son-in-law Johannes Van der Merwe. I believe the local police have given you some details."

"Ja," she said in a heavy Afrikaans accent.

"My main question is your report to the local police about your granddaughter Colleen being sexually assaulted by her stepfather. I believe that was nine years ago when the girl was just ten?"

"Ja," she said again without elaborating.

"What happened?" asked Lazelle.

"Emmie had Colleen when she was just a teenager herself and they lived at home with us. We never knew who the father was. Emmie would not say.

"I brought up Colleen. Emmie was not an active parent. She studied as a paramedic and went to work. Colleen was more my daughter than hers. We were close and she told me everything. I was the one who helped her with her homework. I took her to school and picked her up. I was the one who talked her through the emotional journey of being a little girl in primary school. For eight years, I knew her best and she relied on me more than her mother.

"When Johannes came along Emmie became pregnant quickly and she left our place to live with him. He was already a successful surgeon, and they had a lovely home in Newlands with a beautiful view of Cape Town's Table Mountain. Colleen went to live with them.

"Emmie, Colleen and little Hansie came to see us regularly, mainly when the surgeon was operating. He didn't have much time for us working-class people. I think we went to dinner in his mansion twice at Christmas.

"Colleen had been away from me and in her new environment for I think a year or more, and so she would have been ten years old. Emmie had some other things to do and left her with me for a few days. We talked as we always did but I noticed she was seriously unhappy about something. The best way for me to describe her demeanour is to say she looked disturbed. I asked what was wrong, and she remained silent. Tears flowed and she excused herself. I let it go until the next day.

"To make a long story short, Colleen eventually told me Josh, that's what she called Johannes, was touching her in her private parts. She understood about sex. I asked her how far it had gone if he had penetrated her? She wouldn't answer but said they had been in his bed when Emmie was out with friends. And Emmie was always out and about.

"I told Colleen that was a crime. She was underage and no adult should be grooming her and having sexual activity with a ten-year-old child. It was against the law. I told Emmie about it and my daughter just dismissed the topic as Colleen fantasising. I was so concerned that I reported it to the police.

"When the local police officers came to me, I told them what I have just told you. They had me attend the local station and make a formal written statement. Then they went to the Van der Merwe home and confronted Johannes, in front of Emmie and Colleen. He denied it all, dismissing the allegation as a figment of my imagination. Again, they all had to be interviewed in person at the police station and make formal written statements.

"Emmie was outraged, and apart from an angry exchange with me later she has never spoken to me or her father again. Colleen, obviously instructed by her mother and stepfather, denied that the conversation with me had ever happened. The local police walked away with nothing to go on. And that, Detective Lazelle, is the whole story."

Lazelle thanked her for the information and rang off.

He arranged with the Cape Town police to send the formal written statements. The one from Mrs De Villiers was as she had told Lazelle. They did not take any statement from Colleen and the file contained a note simply saying the girl was ten years old and made no complaint. The others, from Emmie and Johannes Van der Merwe were of more interest. From Emmie the statement read:

> *Cape Town Police... Newlands. 21 April 2010*
> *Statement from Emmie Van der Merwe in the matter of complaint re assault of the child Colleen Van der Merwe by Johannes Van der Merwe*
>
> *I refute entirely my mother's allegation that my daughter Colleen was molested by my husband Johannes Van der Merwe. The child is ten years old and my mother is prone to exaggerate.*
>
> *I have talked with Colleen about this matter, and she has no complaint. She enjoys a close and proper loving relationship with her stepfather. I am happy that we as a family have a normal and comfortable life.*
>
> *Signed Emmie Van der Merwe. (Witnessed by two police officers).*

The statement from Johannes Van der Merwe read:

> *Cape Town Police, Newlands 21 April 2010*
> *Statement from Johannes Van der Merwe in the matter of the complaint re assault of the child Colleen Van der Merwe by Johannes Van der Merwe*
>
> *I deny the allegation by Mrs De Villiers. I have never done anything untoward with my stepdaughter Colleen. I love her as if she was my own child and as a professional surgeon, with a good income, I am privileged to provide for my family comfortably.*

THE INTROSPECTIVE DETECTIVE

Our children, Colleen and Hansie are our entire focus, and we do all that we can to help them grow happily and to have every opportunity to be well educated and able to enjoy a successful life. The accusations from my mother-in-law are motivated by jealousy and a desire to discredit me and steal her grandchildren from us.

Signed Johannes Van der Merwe. (Witnessed by two police officers).

Having read both statements Lazelle questioned the truthfulness of what had happened. Undoubtedly the word of a prominent surgeon would have carried a great deal of weight with the police. The word of a ten-year-old girl perhaps questionable. The complaint made by a grandmother perhaps understandable, but if the girl had exaggerated, what then? In any event, it happened nine years ago and was dismissed by the police at the time.

CHAPTER TWENTY-EIGHT

It had become obvious to Lazelle that the Van der Merwe family was central to solving this murder case. And the one person he wanted to interview next was the thirteen-year-old son, Hansie.

Victorian State law stipulates that if you are under eighteen years of age, police must not formally question you without the parents or an independent person representing the boy being present. Lazelle had every reason to believe the same lawyer, Geoff Wilson, would be that person. The teenager must be given the chance to speak privately with parents or the independent person before being questioned. The interview must be conducted by using language and questions that the young person can understand given their age and maturity.

Lazelle met with DS Kellogg and DC Sam Long to discuss the next steps. Rather than hastily rushing into an interview that would be quickly disrupted by the lawyer, Lazelle suggested they might try to interview some parents of Hansie's friends. If the meetings could be arranged after school, they might possibly include in those family interviews the boys who knew him.

He asked Sam to begin the task of finding out about Hansie's friends by talking to teachers at the boy's secondary private school.

It was one of the finest and most expensive colleges in Melbourne, and Lazelle had every expectation of cooperation from both teachers and parents.

Sam made a phone call to Mr Glasson, the Head of the Middle School at the Kew College, and explained the case they were working on. He agreed to meet the detectives within the hour. Baz Kellogg accompanied her to the main administration building mid-afternoon.

The Middle School comprised years five through eight, and from there the students progressed to the senior school for their final four years prior to a tertiary education… if their marks were good enough and if that was their preference.

"Hansie Van der Merwe is in year eight and doing quite well," the head of school told them. "He is an active student, good at his academic work. He is an exceptional athlete and will do well in our summer all colleges athletics carnival. He is well developed for his age, and he can run the 100 metres in under 12 seconds. He is close to breaking our college record for his age group."

"Who are his friends?" asked Kellogg.

"Let me go and talk to a few of his teachers. They're in class but I can interrupt since this is a police matter."

Baz Kellogg and Sam Long said they would wait, and Mr Glasson left the office. The school was over 150 years old and on high ground so that you could see the city skyline in the not so far distance. The grounds were immaculate, the swimming centre, lawn tennis courts, hockey, football, and soccer fields all superb. Clearly, the boys at this school were privileged and their parents paid high fees for their education.

Eventually the Head came back and gave the detectives the names and addresses of three families and the names of their sons who were friends and in class with Hansie. The boys met socially to do teenage things together outside of school.

Sam Long arranged the three meetings with the nominated families. They deliberately set an appointment for the early evening so that the parents would be home from work and the college boys available to be in the room with them. All three meetings were arranged for this evening. It was explained that the matter was urgent though they did not mention Hansie Van der Merwe. None of the families knew anything about the enquiry.

Lazelle took one of the appointments alone, DS Kellogg and DC Sam Long another and DSC Reed and DC Wells the third.

The interview with the Smythe family conducted by Reed and Wells was of no help. The parents did not have any relationship with the Van der Merwe's, and their son John just seemed to hang out with Hansie, sometimes to meet and ride their bikes along the riverbank and maybe stop for a milkshake. He told them that Hansie's closest friend was Henry Banks. They were in the athletics team together and had much more in common.

Kellogg and Sam Long had more help from the Fleming family. Their son Michael was a close friend of Hansie. The father however, before any questions were asked or answered, demanded to know the reasons for the police visit.

"We are detectives from the Homicide squad," Kellogg answered. "One of the surgeon Johannes Van der Merwe's colleagues in the hospital has been murdered and our enquiry at this stage is broad ranging to try and understand their relationship and what has happened. No one is under suspicion. Otherwise, I can't say more. This is part of an ongoing investigation.

"How can we help?" asked Mr Fleming.

"Did you as a family have any social relationship with the Van der Merwe's?"

"Not really," answered the father. "We just used to talk to one another at sports events. It is compulsory every Saturday morning for the boys to play sport. So, we sometimes met up and said hello on those occasions."

"How close were the boys, Michael and Hansie?"

The mother answered. "The boys were quite friendly. Hansie would come here often but they never had Michael go there. I felt she, the wife, and I can't even remember her name, was stuck up and kept to her own social group outside of college. She never volunteered to do lunch duties or take part in anything to do with the school. They were one of those families you sometimes get here that pay their fees and say that's enough. No need to do anything else. And they let the rest of us work our guts out for their sons and ours."

"What did you guys talk about?" Kellogg asked young Michael in the presence of his mother and father.

"Lots of things. Mainly our sports. AFL football. Hansie had only been introduced to Australian Rules footy in the past two years and I did all I could to get him to barrack for Richmond. I think in the end he has gone with Henry Banks and Essendon."

"Did he tell you much about his family?" asked Sam Long.

"Not really. I once asked why I never went to his place, and he was always welcome at ours. He said his dad was at work as a surgeon. His Mum was always out socialising. His sister Colleen had issues and it was better he came to my house."

As luck would have it, Lazelle had drawn the most productive interview. He sat with the Banks parents, and they called their son Henry, a good friend of Hansie, into the room. Lazelle explained the investigation briefly and asserted most emphatically that this was a broad investigation. He told them that they need not fear being involved in any other way than to answer a few questions now.

"Do you know the Van der Merwe family?" he asked the parents.

Mrs Banks answered. "Yes, but not well. We have been at school events and sat together. Probably they know us best of anyone. I think we have been prepared to understand them and give them more time than others. Johannes is a busy surgeon and not much for general conversation. And if he gets on a subject on interest to him, he has a dogmatic way of expressing his opinions.

"We're Australian through and through and I understand they have only been here two years from a country torn apart by racism, then the abolition of apartheid, and now a ruling class that is disappointing them all. I feel South Africans come here to escape. A lot of their thoughts and opinions are severely hampered by their previous experiences."

Lazelle waited. After a few moments the husband said his piece. "I want to like them, but it is hard. Hansie is always welcome here with Henry because the lad seems to have been through a lot. His school and his friends are the mainstay of his existence. I get nothing from Hansie that gives me the feeling his life at home is fulfilling."

"What do you talk about with Hansie, Henry?" Lazelle asked the son.

"I like Hansie, and he likes me. We are good friends at school and out of hours. What I don't understand is what has happened? I heard your explanation at the start, but we are two thirteen-year-old boys, and you are talking about the murder of a doctor. What have we to do with anything?"

The boy had tested Lazelle with that question. He was thoughtfully seeking a way to answer simply what this was all about. "Let me try to explain. And let me also say that we should all forget television murder mysteries. In real life nothing is simple. My work is asking questions all over the place to try and solve a crime.

"This is a case where a surgical colleague of Mr Van der Merwe, who was operating with him late one night, went on the train home and died because he was stabbed. The last people to see him alive except for the attacker are the surgeon and the team at the hospital.

"Further investigations lead us to want to understand the relationship between the surgeon and the dead man. Also, part of that discovery is to understand the Van der Merwe family and the way they are. We are talking with friends of the family, friends of their children, Colleen and Hansie. It may seem hard to believe, but sometimes we get vital information from something someone says who is quite remote from any crime. Does that help? You are in no way implicated in anything wrong. This is just a meeting where you, or your parents, might have heard Hansie say something that could change the way we understand things."

The boy was thoughtful for what seemed a long time. His parents looked at him inquisitively, for they seemed to instinctively predict that he knew something that would be helpful to the police.

"All Hansie would ever tell me was why I couldn't go to their place. He came here often but I was never welcome there. I did go once or twice for a very short time, mainly for him to pick something up or get some money for us to buy stuff. Usually when I was there, no one else was around.

"He used to say his mother and sister Colleen were not like a real mother and daughter. His mother did not want to grow up and she only ever saw herself as Colleen's sister. And then he said something I didn't really understand like 'they are sister wives.'"

Mr and Mrs Banks audibly drew breath. They had no idea about this and instantly knew what their son was saying. Lazelle quickly put a 'lid on the conversation'.

"Thank you, Henry. Now I will need you to come to the police station and make a formal statement. I will have someone arrange that tomorrow. And I want to end this interview by asking you all to keep this information to yourselves. Okay?"

They all nodded.

Henry Banks made a statement in the presence of his father and DC Dave Wells the very next day. Wells added that to the murder file and confirmed with Lazelle it had been done.

CHAPTER TWENTY-NINE

Baz Kellogg arrived home about 7:30 that evening. His wife Jennifer had packed her things and was ready to leave for Perth. His heart sank when he saw her bags all assembled near the front door.

"When are you going?" he asked.

"I am on a flight tomorrow morning," she replied. "I have ordered a taxi and will stay over with a friend tonight. I thought I may have left before you came home."

"Were you just going to leave without saying goodbye?"

"I left a note on your bedside table."

He looked at her sadly and did not reach out to her. "Who is the friend?" he asked,

"Margaret Jamieson… she is one of our Melbourne consultants and is helpful. She has been through her own break-up and understands the difficulty we are having right now."

"I have not asked you before but perhaps in all honesty now, will you tell me if there is another man in your life?"

"There is no one else. Just my work… like you… my personal life doesn't exist. Perhaps that's what I am trying to find. A balanced life that we can never achieve together with you in the police force."

"If I left would that change things?" he asked.

"Maybe it is too late for us to find out now. I am making a new start in Perth."

"So, this is goodbye and no chance to ever get back together?"

"Read the note I left you."

The taxi beeped and she opened the door. Baz helped her with her bags and before she entered the car, she kissed him lightly on the lips. There were tears in her eyes and his.

He went back indoors and poured a beer. He sat for a while before reading the note she had left on his bedside table.

> My dear Baz,
>
> I know this has been a shock for you and it has not been easy for me. You never asked if there was another man, and I respect you for that. There is no one else. You are the one I fell in love with and married. In the years that followed we gradually became distant from one another.
>
> Your job is my great problem and that is not fair to you. I think you are a wonderful detective and deserve to keep on progressing in that field. But for me it has always been something that prevents us having a close relationship and as you know, I have not wanted to have a family while this was our way of life. And eventually, I do want to be a mother and to have children.
>
> I don't know what the future holds. I am travelling to the other side of Australia to find out. I will call you when I am in Perth sometime in the next few weeks. Perhaps if we talk by phone out of hours, we might help one another.
>
> I have only ever really loved you Baz. I am sorry to hurt you now,
>
> Jennifer xxx

CHAPTER THIRTY

Lazelle invited the four other detectives and Georgie to breakfast at McDonald's the next morning at 8:30 am. He, Kellogg, Reed, Wells, Long and Georgie sat in a corner booth where bacon and egg McMuffins, fries, pancakes, maple syrup and coffee were all provided at the leader's expense. They were surprised.

They swapped notes from their various previous interviews. After that they all waited for the wisdom that Lazelle was famous for. His deep thinking and considered opinions often turned the case in an instant. Yet again he surprised them.

"This is a tough one," said Lazelle. "You all know the facts so far. You have all heard the conjecture from the recent interviews. I want your thoughts… I especially want the female opinions first. Sam, what do you think? After that, Georgie, give me your thoughts. Nothing is off the table and nothing you say can be considered silly. Let's have some free thinking here."

Samantha Long considered her response. She was surprised and caught off-guard. They sipped coffee as she took her time to reply. "I believe Johannes Van der Merwe has groomed and abused his stepdaughter, Colleen, as a minor and has now taken her as a second wife.

The mother knows it. I believe Hansie knows it. This is behind the attack on Dr Grace. I think Colleen told Grace about the situation she was in."

Georgie added. "I think Sam has it right. In my view the attacker was one of the Van der Merwe family. And I think Dr Grace recognised his attacker."

Lazelle waited for others to say something. He was worried about his right-hand man Baz Kellogg. Something was terribly wrong. Nevertheless, Kellogg quietly, and almost reluctantly, offered his opinion. "I agree that something has happened in the Van der Merwe family. Nobody is saying they are upset with their situation unless in the intimate discussions she had with Dr Grace, Colleen told him all. But then how does that bring about a motive to kill?"

DSC John Reed offered his opinion. "Let's say Colleen had 'spilled the beans'… why would she? She has been in this situation for many years, since childhood. She is now a consenting adult. She is part of a modern wealthy family that has everything they need. She has no other lover. She has no interest elsewhere. Why was she talking to Grace? Did she have an affair with him? He was a man torn apart by his own inhibitions. Why a burner phone? Grace's own wife cheated on him. I don't get how this comes together at all."

Dave Wells added, "I agree. There is no clear motive. I do not believe Dr Grace knew his attacker. The chances were high he would not die from a random thin spike stabbing. If he had survived, he would have pointed us straight to the assailant."

Lazelle nodded appreciatively and continued eating his McMuffin, allowing a long silence to hold everyone in suspense. They ate and they waited.

"I think you are all right in parts," he said. "Colleen was groomed and has been in a sexual relationship with her stepfather since she was ten. That is a crime the South African police should have discovered. Since she has been in Australia the past two years, she could claim to be a consenting adult. I believe her mother is probably out and about with other men. It might well be that she chooses to accept what is happening between her husband and Colleen and is content to live happily on her husband's wealth.

"Hansie knows about it all and is embarrassed. He is 13, an adolescent boy maturing rapidly. It must be a very difficult time for him.

"Dr Grace has my sympathy, not just because of his death but because of the way he lived. I have some understanding of being a quiet, withdrawn man. We are not all from families where sharing and caring was the norm. I think Dr Grace migrated here to please his Australian wife and was probably missing his original home. I don't believe he knew his wife was cheating.

"I tend to agree that the attacker was not known to Dr Grace. The helmet, Lycra body suit and raincoat camouflaged the identity of the person. The likelihood that the wound would not be fatal was high. So, it is difficult to understand the attack. As some of you have asked, 'what is the motive'?

"I find it hard to believe that Colleen was having a sexual relationship with Grace, and I do find it plausible she may have eventually told him of her situation with her stepfather. That probably became a serious conversation in the last month... hence the burner phone. The fact that most calls were made in the few days before his death suggests something urgent was happening. What did Grace fear might happen to the girl? What was he planning to do about it?"

They all considered these thoughts silently. Then Lazelle outlined the next actions.

"We are at a stage where we need to interview formally both Colleen and the boy Hansie again. That must be done carefully and by the book because he is underage."

With those instructions they left the breakfast meeting to start work.

CHAPTER THIRTY-ONE

The body of Dr Grace was released for a funeral and burial. A coronial inquest would be scheduled in a few weeks with evidence from the post-mortem and supporting information from the police. Anne Grace would not receive the life insurance payout until the case was solved or the police had at least cleared Mrs Grace as a suspect. Lazelle was not prepared to do that yet.

The funeral was held in the Church of England chapel at the Grammar School the children attended. Anne Grace, her parents, her daughters, and many other adult friends from school were all there. Most of the surgical teams with whom the anaesthetist had worked attended, including Johannes Van der Merwe and his stepdaughter Colleen. Emmie did not come.

The service was sombre. The chaplain clearly had no idea about the deceased but read his eulogy from notes provided. Anne, Abbie, and Josie were tearful, and sobbing at times. Anne's parents were unmoved. Otherwise, nothing untoward happened. Colleen seemed in control of her emotions and the surgeon remained indifferent.

Lazelle and Kellogg were observers at the funeral. As people were dispersing afterwards, Dr Garry Johnson approached the detectives.

"I wonder if I might have a word. In your offices please," asked the doctor.

Within the hour, Dr Johnson, Lazelle, and Kellogg were seated in an interview room at Homicide HQ. Kellogg asked if they could videotape what was said and formalise the proceedings. Johnson agreed.

"After our previous interview, I thought hard and long before coming to you about this matter. It bothers me that I might know something important. But it sounds so fantastic. I didn't always know much about Francis. He was hard to read. So, I am just not sure what he meant."

"What do you know?" asked Lazelle.

"Very recently he told me that a young woman had confided in him. She was a troubled girl who had been sexually exploited by a member of her family from the age of ten and it was still going on, though the girl was now nineteen. Francis didn't ever say the name of the family.

"I asked him how he became involved, and he declined to answer. He said the girl wanted out of the family and to live a new life. He wanted to help her leave home. I asked him if he was romantically involved with the girl and he said no. In the last two weeks he became increasingly nervous. He stopped talking to me."

"Have you formed any opinion about who the family was?"

"No, and it would be foolish for me to hazard a guess. I wondered though whether it has something to do with Van der Merwe. And in a way, I think the only reason he said anything to me was to make sure someone else knew... just in case..."

"In case of what?"

"I don't know. But in view of what has happened..."

Lazelle thought for a moment. "I cannot understand how you have kept this from us for nearly two weeks now."

"I know," the doctor agreed. "I should have said something sooner. But at least I have told you now. I still don't know what was right and what was wrong. The one thing I do know is that Francis Grace was a shy, good man who kept to himself. He had no friends I knew of, and his only associations were with people at work. That is why what he told me was so unusual."

CHAPTER THIRTY-TWO

Lazelle served formal written notice by email to the Van der Merwe's and their lawyers, Patterson & Partners. It said that within 48 hours, they would require Colleen for further questioning and that it was crucial to the case that the boy Hansie should also be interviewed.

By that afternoon the law firm responded on behalf of the family seeking to discover on what grounds these interviews were necessary. They explicitly objected to the boy being interviewed. They asserted that the family was being subject to police harassment. They also asked for the transcripts of all the family interviews so far. That was the legal right of an interviewee.

Although he regularly kept his boss, Detective Superintendent Pizzey up to date with the case by succinct emailed written reports, Lazelle knew that this situation must be discussed with him in person. He phoned Pizzey's office and was given a time within the hour to meet.

"How is it going DI Lazelle?" The Super was mostly formal with his subordinates, as he expected them to be with him.

"I think you know most of what has happened during the investigation in this case Sir." He showed Pizzey the exchange of emails with the law firm. "No-one in the family is aware that we have circumstantial evidence of the grooming and sexual activity between the surgeon Van der Merwe and his stepdaughter Colleen. We have heard from others that this started in South Africa when she was just ten, and is happening even now, though the girl is nineteen and might claim to be a consenting adult."

"Just a minute," interrupted Pizzey. "If she is an unwilling partner at any age that constitutes rape."

"Yes Sir." Lazelle conceded. "But there has been no such complaint and that is what we need to find out here. I am sure the Grace killing has to do with the fact Colleen told him about her situation and he was probably going to do something. He certainly provided the girl with a burner phone to call him if she needed help. We believe the boy knows all about what was happening. These interviews are probably our last chance to get someone from inside the family to tell us the truth.

"I suggest we respond to the law firm along the lines of 'further clarification of the relationship between the girl and Dr Grace, and to talk to the boy about activities in his household that may have a bearing on the case.' Will that be okay Sir?"

"Go ahead... I have complete faith in you." The Super knew full well how efficient his Detective Inspector was.

Lazelle framed the email to Patterson & Partners. It included attachments of the transcripts of the formal interviews with the surgeon, his wife and stepdaughter.

Knowing they had no other option, the firm agreed to the interviews, and said that the lawyer Geoff Wilson, accompanied by Ms Brittany Wallace, a Senior Counsel and leading advocate, would be in attendance. The lawyers pointed out that the law required that Hansie must be afforded time to consult with and be properly briefed by his parents and the lawyers as to his rights during the proposed interview. They asserted the right that all questions must be appropriate to his age and state of maturity. They were to be given 48 hours to consult before the interviews.

Lazelle agreed to hold the interviews on Monday. He knew that by then he would have heard from the forensic lab about the bikes and Lycra suit.

CHAPTER THIRTY-THREE

"I want you to keep an eye on Emmie Van der Merwe," Lazelle asked Sam Long. "Can you watch her movements during tonight and tomorrow night? She's a party animal so we can assume she will be out and about on a Friday and Saturday. Take a photographer with you and try to get shots of the people she is with. I know it's a lot to ask."

"Yes sir," the young DC responded. Though she sounded enthusiastic, her weekend plans with her boyfriend were now shattered. To appease him for all the long hours she was working, they had planned a romantic dinner with all the trimmings during and afterwards. Though Sam was a very dedicated member of the team and proud to have been promoted into the Homicide squad so quickly, it was obviously going to be a commitment with its downside so far as time and quality of personal life were concerned. She called her partner. He was most unimpressed that their weekend was about to be ruined.

On the Friday night, Emmie Van der Merwe, looking resplendent in designer fashion clothes and accessories, left home around 7 pm by taxi. She went to the southside riverbank in the city and met three other people in a chic bar. The others were two women and a man of similar ages. Forties, Sam guessed, probably all with teenage children.

She wondered whether they were friends made amongst parents at Hansie's school. Discreetly, the photographer captured the moments.

After an hour or so, the subject excused herself and walked across Princes Bridge and up Collins Street to a well-known high-end restaurant. Sam and the photographer followed her to reception where they saw her acknowledge and wave to a man waiting for her at a table for two. Though they had no reservation, Sam, and her colleague were shown to another table where they sat for a few moments, she supposedly looking at the menu, while he photographed the pair. Sam then apologised profusely, and they prepared to leave the restaurant. She could only imagine what would be said in the squad room if they had eaten and run up a fancy bill there.

From what little they saw, Emmie Van der Merwe knew the man, and he was probably younger than her. They were not overtly romantic but obviously were comfortable in each another's company.

Emmie and the man left the restaurant around 10 pm and went to another wine bar for further drinks. Again, photos were taken.

At around 11 pm Emmie took a taxi the short distance home alone. Sam and the photographer called it a night, and she went to her boyfriend's place to try to make up for lost time together.

On Saturday evening, Emmie Van der Merwe left home again around 7 pm. It was a balmy evening, and her dress was informal. There was no stepping out tonight. She took a taxi from a rank nearby. Sam and the photographer followed her in the unmarked police car to a residence in Hawthorn. She entered the building at around 7:25 pm and did not reappear until 11 pm when a taxi she must have ordered was waiting to drive her home.

After she had left, Sam knocked on the door of the residence, with the photographer hidden and ready to take a shot of the person that answered. He was the same man who had dined with Emmie Van der Merwe the previous evening. Sam excused herself for being at a wrong address and they left.

The photos were emailed to the team on Sunday morning. Kellogg immediately phoned Lazelle and identified the mystery man as the young surgical registrar, Anton Delaney.

CHAPTER THIRTY-FOUR

"This case is insane," said Kellogg to Lazelle, obviously and uncharacteristically uptight. "During the surgery, Delaney is the one who made the crack about a girlfriend running hot and cold. Van der Merwe makes a snide comment to Grace about emotions, not knowing that Delaney was probably talking about Emmie, the surgeon's wife. God help us to know where this will end. We've moved on from a pool boy maybe knocking off his lover's husband to the surgeon or one of his family doing the job to hide child molestation and rape allegations. And now how about the surgical registrar and Emmie conniving to do the deed?"

"Why though?" asked Lazelle. He was sure this woman was into other men. "Perhaps this explains why she doesn't care that her husband is sleeping with her daughter. You're right, this case is confounding."

On Sunday lunchtime, Lazelle went to his son Andrew's place for a proper Sunday roast. Andrew and his wife Lily lived in a lovely upmarket home as befitted the 38-year-old banker and his family.

Their two boys, Johnny, and Keith were 11 and 9 years old and at a stage where whenever they saw Poppa Robin, they were excited. They were all over him with hugs and kisses.

"Hi Poppa," said Johnny. "Love you Poppa"," said Keith.

"What have you been up to boys?" he asked.

"Nothing much… just school and stuff," said Johnny.

"I played football yesterday in the Under 10 team. We won," Keith yelled out loudly.

Lazelle gave them both more hugs and said, "I'm very proud of you both."

"Sing us 'the little shirt me mother made for me," asked Johnny excitedly.

"Yes do," shouted Keith at the top of his voice.

"All right," said Poppa Robin. Then in his rough falsetto and most babyish voice, he began:

> "I remember the day that I was born.
> It was on a very cold and frosty morn.
> The doctor said I was a chubby chap and
> the nurse she placed me on her lap.
> Then she washed me all over I remember.
> And after powder-puffing me, you see.
> She placed me on the table near the fender in…"

(he held the note for a very long time) …

> "… the little shirt me mother made for me. Tiddly Pom."

The 'Tiddly Pom' was sung with a flourish, hands outstretched; a truly vaudeville ending that the grandsons knew and expected; an uncharacteristic pose for the usually serious detective.

The boys clapped and laughed. So did Poppa Robin. "Thanks Poppa," they both shouted as they happily retreated to their own rooms and their laptops for amusement. Poppa was fun.... but they had better things to do.

Lily was in the kitchen doing the vegetables, green beans, carrots, and peas. Andrew was roasting a chicken in the BBQ that was installed on their deck. His father joined him. While his son was basting the bird, both men talked with a beer in hand.

"I heard you singing to the boys Dad," said Andrew. "It brings back memories. You used to sing that to me. How did that song ever come about?"

"I think it is an old Irish folksong from well before the second world war. I guess my grandfather heard it as a soldier during the war and sang it to my dad. So, my dad sang it to me when I was little, and really, it was one of the few times my father ever laughed and was funny. For me, that was a special time. Perhaps you'll get to sing it to your grandchildren. They both chuckled at the prospect.

Andrew spooned more of the roast juices over the chicken breast and then shuffled the separate pan of roast potatoes to make sure they weren't stuck.

"How are you going personally, Dad? I worry about you. It seems to be all work and no play."

Lazelle found himself a little annoyed by the question. He didn't answer.

"C'mon Dad. Talk to me. You know we are here for you. You have never really talked with me... never shared your feelings... and here we are both getting older."

After a few moments, Robin Lazelle said, "I know your mother told you some things. It was in my nature to leave it at that. Anyway... maybe I should share with you my side of the story.

"My father, your grandfather, John, was an only child and brought up in a village in Essex by a mother who was widowed early, because her husband eventually died from war injuries. She was awarded a small military widow's pension and spent most of it drowning her sorrows in gin. My father found himself caring for an alcoholic mother, and only managed to put food on the table by leaving school and taking up carpentry at the age of 14. He worked as an apprentice on basic wages. By his late teens he was a competent tradesman.

"My grandmother died from organ failure caused by her alcoholism. As a child and teenager, Dad experienced emotional deprivation but was nevertheless dutiful in providing for his mother and always worked hard. He was a respected employee.

"Your grandmother, Irene came from London. She was an only child too. Her family was well-to-do. Her father was a professional land surveyor working for the government. Though they lived comfortably, he spent most of his leisure time gambling either in the betting shops or at the track. My grandma was a downtrodden woman with little to say. Mum grew up as an only, lonely child.

"Mum and Dad met in London quite by chance in their early twenties. They quickly learned about their common backgrounds and fast became friends in need of each other. They married in London and had me and my younger sister Cathy. Seeking a new life, we all emigrated to Australia. You never knew Cathy because she was deaf and then died from a brain tumour when I was just a teenager. Because she was deaf, our household did not speak but just signed. Our household was silent... soundless... sounds disturbed us. Silence was comfortable.

"I was brought up by parents who had never shared, who kept to themselves. Even after Cathy died, we signed and never talked. We never really communicated with one another... the idea of love and compassion was absent until I met your mother. As a child, I guess I had to adapt and survive by becoming just like my parents. Even now, I am withdrawn. I don't enjoy social life and apart from my work,

I don't know what I would do. After your mother died, only my work has given me whatever self-esteem I have. Her loss was devastating then and I miss her even more now."

Andrew was silent for a while, and then said, "Thanks, Dad, for sharing. Mum had told me most of what you have just said, but perhaps the fact that you're telling me about your feelings now will be helpful."

They sipped their beers.

"Andrew, just being here with you, Lily and the boys for lunch is a great comfort to me. This is a social family life that I enjoy. I can be myself. But you shouldn't worry. I am doing okay. I lead a team of good people at work, and they like and support me.

"I guess the days ahead are a little daunting," he continued. "I am nearing retirement. I don't know what to do if I don't keep working. I don't know how to feel about old age without your mother. I know there are thousands of men in my position and going through the same thing. I have no right to feel sorry for myself. It's just a sort of crossroads. I will be fine. Don't worry."

"I do worry that your life is mostly work," said Andrew. "It must be stressful a lot of the time. How are you handling that?"

"I'm okay. In the middle of an investigation, we go without sleep. I have a few aches and pains. Maybe I'm not as fit as I was. A little breathless from time to time. But my job is about thinking and seeking the truth. I promise you; I'm not out there physically wrestling with the bad guys."

Andrew lifted the lid on the roast chicken. Then he said, "Dad. To be honest not one of us is sure about what comes next. We can only believe that things will work out. Meanwhile, I think this chicken and the roast spuds are ready."

He called the boys and Lily brought out the greens. Andrew carved the bird and they all served themselves, generously filling their plates. The men drank beer, the others soft drinks. As a family, they sat outside on the deck on a beautiful sunny day and enjoyed Sunday lunch together.

At home, Lazelle ate a light salad for the evening meal and was grateful for the substantial Sunday lunch with Andrew, Lily, and the boys.

He was sad that Andrew had been an only child. It wasn't for want of trying but they weren't able to have more children. He was sad that Andrew knew no real love or interest from his grandparents because they were so distant and withdrawn. Both had passed away in their seventies from complications of cardiovascular disease. That was twelve and fourteen years ago now. Lazelle felt they both died from broken hearts. Their common life experiences in dysfunctional families, having no siblings, losing Cathy; they were never happy so far as he could remember. His sadness when his parents passed away was that he couldn't feel any emotions at all. There was nothing there.

He desperately hoped that he had been a better father than that for Andrew. He knew that Jane was a wonderful Mum. In his heart he felt she had made sure that he was a good dad even if she took over doing most of what he should have done but was too busy. Certainly, he was grateful that Andrew and Lily and the boys were so loving and kind, though he wondered if he deserved their care and concern.

The conversation with his son caused him to reflect on his feelings about the future. Work was the constant and when he retired, he knew life would be substantially different. Apart from his son, daughter-in-law and two grandsons he had no-one else and no other interests.

It caused him to panic sometimes, inside not outwardly. His feelings were internalised and rarely shown or shared. The exceptions were when Cathy died. That was long ago. He was just a teenager and he cried many times after losing her. And of course, the feelings he shared with his lovely wife, Jane. Her loss was devastating when it happened and sometimes, he felt even worse and missed her more now. She was gone and he was alone. He felt very alone. Lost really.

His was the same situation as that of many people, most of whom simply moved on and found other reasons to live successfully in their later years. He knew that was the right thing to do. Intellectually he could think reasonably, but that didn't last long. At his core, deep in his gut, he was afraid. Most of the time he felt singularly depressed about the new world of an introspective detective nearing retirement.

He cringed at the thought of having to take up bowls or play golf. That didn't interest him at all. He couldn't see himself playing bridge or joining a social club. He really was never comfortable amongst a lot of people. There was never a feeling that he should find another partner, No one could replace Jane.

He reflected on faith and a belief in God. Babies were born into families all over the world and simply indoctrinated into the religion of their fathers. Whether Christian, Jewish, Muslim, Buddhist, Hindu whatever, the children had no say. Lazelle fundamentally believed that each religion was inspired by the prophet for whom it was created. All the prophets were basically trying to teach love for one another and a respect for the rights and dignity of all. They provided foundations for viable communities. All religions should get on because they all had the same aims.

He decried that a small minority of people who were extremists perverted the teachings of the prophets and in all religions such bigots took their twisted interpretations into places they should not go.

Lazelle was born into a Christian family, so far as ticking the boxes on the Australian Government census form was concerned. However, his parents didn't go to church. Apart from religious instruction at school he had no exposure to Christianity.

He felt envious of people who through sheer faith were supported by their beliefs. He was envious that they thought there was an afterlife with better things to come. He just couldn't see it... when your time was up that was it.

He sat back comfortably in his favourite chair and sipped his single malt Scotch.

CHAPTER THIRTY-FIVE

Lazelle was deeply troubled that this case was so difficult and had gone on so long. Usually things were a great deal simpler, the culprit more obvious, the motive plain, and the deceased, killed because of emotions, anger, jealousy, greed... all reasons that were not hard to find and explain. But this Francis Grace murder? It was baffling.

The interviews that had been agreed for Monday would take place. The lawyers argued that Mrs Van der Merwe would not be available this day. Some other time had to be arranged.

Of today's interviews, the boy Hansie was first at Lazelle's insistence. They sat in a confined windowless interview room, Lazelle, and Kellogg one side of the table, the boy, Wilson, and Ms Wallace SC on the other. The protocols were observed for the recording to identify the participants, time of interview and the introductory explanation of the boy's rights.

Lazelle knew he had to be at the top of his game. This was a once only chance. And he worried that with such a competent counsel present, the boy would be advised not to answer several of his questions. Ms Wallace was famous for her fine intellect and effective courtroom advocacy.

It was unusual that a top barrister would find the time to attend a police interview. Then again, Van der Merwe could afford to pay.

"What do you know about Colleen and her relationship with your father?" he asked directly.

"They are close," was the rehearsed answer.

"You are under oath at this interview," Lazelle insisted. "Did you know your father and Colleen have been sleeping together from when she was quite young?"

The boy looked at the lawyers. Ms Wallace spoke, "asked and answered."

Lazelle continued. "I have heard from others that you once told a friend your mother and Colleen were 'sister wives' to your father. Is that so?" And as if to anticipate the woman lawyer's objection, he added, "that has not been asked and answered."

"Hansie can refuse to answer that question," she said.

"You're right," Lazelle conceded, "but there will come a time in a court of law when he does not have the right to refuse to answer unless he is protecting his own guilt. Is that the case here Hansie?"

The boy looked flustered and was not handling this situation well despite the protection of his high-priced lawyers.

"Hansie, way back when Colleen was just a ten-year-old girl, your grandmother complained to the South African Police because your sister told her she was being sexually assaulted by your father. That charge went away because everyone in your family denied it. You were too young to be involved, I get that. But you know that sexual relationship never stopped. Your father is sleeping with both your mother and your half-sister. That is the truth is it not?"

"I don't know," came another rehearsed answer.

"Why have you repeatedly asked to visit your friends at their homes and never wanted them to come to your house? What is wrong at your house?"

"My father works... he's never home. Mum goes her own way and is not home much either. Colleen has university. My house is not like my friends'. They have a proper family. I wish I did too."

"So, you are unhappy about your family and the way you live together?"

"Yes," the boy answered emphatically and before any lawyers could object.

"How close are you to your father? Do you love him, does he tell you he loves you? Do you do much together?"

"No." That was the short answer with no embellishment.

"How close are you to your mother?" Lazelle asked.

Hansie paused... "she wishes I had never been born and only stays with my dad for the money."

The lawyers were flabbergasted. That was never a rehearsed answer.

Ms Wallace immediately interrupted. "This is out of line. These are questions, the lad should not answer. You are entrapping him to put down his family. What are the questions that are relevant to the case?"

Lazelle ignored her and asked his next question. "Did Colleen tell you anything about what she and Dr Grace were talking about before he was murdered?

The boy took his time. "Colleen told me she liked Dr Grace. He gave her hope for a better future. I feel she might have told him her darkest secrets."

"Why do you say that?"

"Colleen told me that Dr Grace was going to help her get away," he said. "And she didn't want me to be left alone with my parents."

The boy seemed flustered and clearly wanted this to end.

"That's enough," said Ms Wallace. "This interview is over."

"One last question... a change of subject. The four bicycles we took to our forensic laboratories have been examined and I have their report. Yours is the most beat up. Why is that?"

"I often drop my bike on the ground. Me and my mates all do."

"The lab found a single spoke in your front wheel has been replaced. When did that happen?"

Hansie thought for a moment. "My mother took the bike to have it serviced and it was missing for a couple of days. I guess I had broken a spoke."

"Can you remember when?"

"I know the bike was gone Wednesday and Thursday the week before last," the boy replied. "I needed it for Wednesday after school and it was missing. I asked Mum and she said it needed a service. It was back in the garage Thursday afternoon because I had sports training and used it then."

"Where would she take the bike?"

"I guess the same place we bought them. I don't know where exactly, but my mother can tell you."

CHAPTER THIRTY-SIX

After Hansie left, Colleen was brought to the interview room. Otherwise, the personnel were the same. Lazelle prefaced his questions with a long introduction.

"We are twelve days into the investigation of this murder. We have evidence from people who assert that there was a problem between your stepfather and Dr Grace. We believe the problem was that you, Colleen, had become close to the victim and told him of your child molestation and the ongoing sexual abuse by your stepfather.

"Your stepfather knew enough to believe Dr Grace was a threat to your family. If Grace reported what he knew, it would be terrible for you all. However, I don't think he was going to do that. I believe he was willing and ready to help you leave home to get a better life, an independent life. I think the burner phone was part of that plan for you to be able to talk with him and act anonymously.

"I further believe your mother knew about it and doesn't want anything to change. We have come to a time where events are about to collide. We have so much information that demonstrates your family is actively obstructing this investigation."

Ms Wallace interrupted him. "You have the girl here for questioning. This is not the time for a lecture, so I suggest you begin."

Lazelle continued. "Colleen. This is your last chance to be very honest with me and to help us find who it was that murdered your friend. And trust me, I know he was your friend and trying to help you. I believe there was nothing untoward about your relationship with Dr Grace.

"The last time we spoke, your lawyer advised you not to tell us what you had talked to Dr Grace about and what he knew that probably was the reason for his death. That question will be answered here or in court. It leads to a motive for murder. Now I am going to ask you again, what did you tell him, how much did he know?"

This introduction had brought tears to her eyes. Colleen was quietly upset but in firm control of her feelings.

"I am going to remind my client that she is not obliged to answer any questions and can refuse to do so at any time," Ms Wallace said quietly sensing the difficult position the girl was in.

Lazelle waited. Colleen considered her position. She drew a deep breath and began.

"Here is what I am prepared to say to help you. First and foremost, whatever happened in South Africa, no matter what you think, is not something I will talk about in this interview. We are in Australia now and I am at an age of consent. Let's assume… I repeat assume for the moment that there is a sexual relationship between my stepfather and me here in Australia. We are not related by blood, and I have never claimed to anyone, including Dr Grace, that I have been raped."

The lawyers looked proud. She was doing so well.

Colleen continued. "However, I understand your interest in what Dr Grace and I meant to each other. So let me tell you how I see it.

"The relationship I have with my stepfather is disdainful. He gets what he wants, and he doesn't 'give a damn'. He married my mother who as I am sure Hansie will also tell you, doesn't want to be a Mum and wants to be a young woman who never grows up. She is the sort of woman you could easily pick up in a bar. And for a daughter to say that about her mother is significant.

"When Francis and I became closer and closer through conversation and comparing our emotions and feelings at different stages of life, he despaired that such things had happened and continued to happen to me. He told me he absolutely hated Josh and I guess that might have showed. And Josh was really scared of what he might do. Although he didn't know what I had told Francis, he knew enough to accuse me of wanting to leave home.

"Francis was actively helping me to prepare to do just that. As I am only a student, he would have financed it. He said it was an opportunity for him to do something good and worthwhile. He didn't think much of himself and was miserable in his own life. He felt distant from his wife and guilty about the way he was failing his daughters… in other words, his was just another family that might be described as dysfunctional.

"Now you who judge, detectives and lawyers, have a think about your own families. There are many in this city who have complicated relationships. Who are we to judge? Perhaps, your family is one of them."

Lazelle was impressed. Both the children of the Van der Merwe's were obviously very bright and articulate. Especially Colleen. Her answers had been exceptional and beautifully worded. Lazelle thought them both sincere. That surely was not a product of coaching by lawyers entirely. There was a depth of personal feeling in it all.

"Who do you think is responsible for Dr Grace's death?" he asked.

"I honestly don't know," she replied.

"You may have wondered why we seized all the bicycles from your garage. It is not known, and we have not said it elsewhere, but the murderer rode a bike that we know had fallen over and would have scratches. Only Hansie's bike is knocked about a lot and has had a spoke in his front wheel replaced."

Colleen was aghast. "You can't be serious. Hansie is no killer. He wouldn't harm a fly and certainly wouldn't hurt anyone I cared about. In our family you must understand the only reason he and I survive is because Hansie and I look out for each other. One of my great problems in moving away from home is to leave him all alone to cope with that pair."

"I am grateful for your time Colleen. I feel that what you have said helps me a great deal."

At the end of the interviews Lazelle spoke with both lawyers and they assured him that Emmie Van der Merwe would be available for interview the following morning. Lazelle said he would send a marked police car to pick her up and bring her to HQ. The lawyers objected, citing this would damage her reputation in the neighbourhood, and instead undertook to bring her to the meeting themselves. Lazelle agreed.

Apart from the analysis of the bicycles, the forensics report also included comments about Emmie's full body Lycra suit. It said that the suit had been washed and scrubbed. There were no blood stains. However, on the inside of the right-hand sleeve there was a very faint dark stain that was not entirely washed away, and that the laboratory could not identify. The lab supervisor's advice was that they would continue testing to identify the stain. It was not something they had seen before.

CHAPTER THIRTY-SEVEN

Kellogg called Anton Delaney. He didn't say why or what they knew but that they needed further information from him. He agreed to be interviewed the following day. Kellogg offered to pick Delaney up, but the man promised to appear at the assigned time using his own transport.

Before going home that evening, Lazelle asked Kellogg to join him in the tearoom. No one else was there so they had a chance to speak alone.

"C'mon Baz... you have to tell me what's wrong," Lazelle said. "I'm not asking because of anything to do with work... I am just concerned about you. And perhaps talking to me will help."

"I guess I can tell you, but it is personal," Kellogg replied anxiously.

"You can tell me... it is between us."

"Jennifer has left me and gone to head up her firm's office in Perth."

Lazelle's eyes widened, but he waited and did not say anything more.

"She does not want me to follow her," Kellogg added. "Our marriage has been falling apart because of both our jobs. She sees no future in it ever improving while I am a policeman. I want to be with her. I even suggested I would leave the police force, but she won't hear of that.

She knows my job is important to me. So, we are separated for now. There is no one else, she assures me about that. Going to Perth is a fresh start for her to see where this might go as a new beginning."

Lazelle was genuinely upset for his colleague. "I am so sorry to hear that Baz. It is hard. Do you need time to perhaps stop and think, maybe a few days to go and see her?"

"No. We'll talk on the phone. I haven't called her because she said she would call first in a week or so and it has only been a few days."

They stood together. Lazelle patted his partner, awkwardly but nevertheless affectionately, on the shoulder. Becoming a detective, losing yourself in the processes of solving crime and spending so many hours away from loved ones, provided no real benefit towards a stable family life. In fact, quite the opposite… it could be very destructive to oneself and one's family.

CHAPTER THIRTY-EIGHT

Emmie Van der Merwe was first. Lazelle guessed that she had been in touch with Delaney and they both knew they were being interviewed the same day. They might have guessed that their liaison had been found out. As Lazelle surmised, that was for them both to 'sweat over'.

With the formalities out of the way, and again in the presence of lawyers Ms Wallace and Mr Williams, her interview with Lazelle and Kellogg began.

"We've done this before," said Lazelle, "and the very fact that these interviews keep repeating themselves is testimony that you have been withholding information that is crucial to this case. I hope this time you will understand the gravity of your situation. I believe the answer to Dr Grace's murder lies squarely within your family group.

"So let us start again. What is your sexual relationship with your husband and what do you know about his sexual relationship with your daughter?"

"You don't have to answer that," said Ms Wallace.

Emmie Van der Merwe declined to comment.

"What do you know about Colleen's relationship with Dr Grace?"

"I know she trusted the man and had befriended him. There was a continuing friendship and anything else I know, has been mainly what you have told me."

"Do you know what Colleen told Dr Grace?"

"No."

"From our surveillance and what your children have said, you are a woman about town. You don't want to be a mother and you do enjoy the social life. What do you say?"

"I know I look selfish and uninterested in my children and husband. Perhaps that is fair comment. I grew up in an ordinary but strict Afrikaans family. My father was a tradesman. We had enough but not much. I always wanted more. When I was a teenager, I became infatuated with an older very wealthy married man who lavished gifts and money upon me. We had an affair and he promised the world, but when I became pregnant, he couldn't run away fast enough. He paid me a monthly allowance, he said for Colleen's upbringing. But it was also to keep me quiet.

"It became obvious that I had some extra money, so I told my parents I had won a bursary to train as a paramedic. When I was qualified and went to work, I exaggerated the salary. The older man kept paying Colleen's allowance until I was with Johannes. His life went on without any hint of scandal. No one knows who Colleen's father is… I promised the man never to tell and I have kept that promise. I have never told anyone. Not even Colleen.

"Of course, being with Johannes the money kept rolling in. I could have anything I wanted. After we had Hansie, we married, and Colleen and I moved into his lavish and very expensive home. She was about seven years old. As a kid she would jump into bed with us. He read her bedtime stories. I knew they seemed close. But it was just lovely family stuff. I thought he was the ideal father for her. I felt lucky. We were happy.

"As a paramedic I had to take my share of nightshifts. When I came home sometimes, I found Colleen asleep with Josh and I would wake her and take her to her own bed. Perhaps I am not as perceptive as most, but I never suspected anything was wrong. Colleen never looked unhappy. She never said anything to me.

"When she was around ten years old, she told my mother that Josh was abusing her, and Mum called the police. That's the first I really knew anything about the possibility of my husband sexually abusing Colleen. We told the police it was all a figment of the girl's imagination, and I then told her to stop telling lies."

Emmie stopped and was clearly emotional. "But in my gut, I knew they weren't lies. I was ashamed of what had happened. I was ashamed that I had failed her as a mother... I was in a family that would always be well-off because of my husband's success. We had money enough to do what I wanted. And the kids were well-off too.

"Within a few days of the police visit, the interviews, and depositions, I had an enormous row with Josh. I got Colleen alone and asked her more about what was happening. She didn't say much... I think he got to her. Anyway, that put a wedge between us. Our marriage was never the same again.

"I started to drink a lot, party more and became distant from Colleen. It is unfair but I especially resented Hansie whom I identified as the son of the man who was raping my daughter. I know that is wrong, but it is a feeling I can't get over.

"It sounds awful... I stayed with Josh and turned a blind eye because of the luxurious life I was living and the determination never to go back to having less. I don't sleep with him much anymore... it might happen but not often. Colleen has always had her own room, but I know they get together if he says that's what he wants. It has become a way of life that I believe each of the four of us have come to accept. It would have stayed like that except for Dr Grace."

The room was silent for some seconds that seemed like minutes. No one could say much more, such had been the outpouring from Emmie.

"Do you have other sexual relationships?" asked Lazelle.

"Yes, from time to time. There have been a few but I don't form any lasting relationships that would interrupt the way I live with my husband and children now."

"You have been seen with the surgical registrar on your husband's operating team, Anton Delaney?"

The woman showed no surprise. Clearly, she and he had worked out they had been seen together.

"So, what have you both been talking about these past few days?" asked Lazelle.

"The situation my family is facing. The Grace killing. Colleen wanting to get out of our family. My son Hansie... my failings as a mother."

"And yet you don't want to change. You're a woman about town not wanting to be a mother. Both of your children have said that about you. It is not a great endorsement of your parenting."

"I know."

"What was it that you think Dr Grace was going to do that would so terribly upset your family situation?"

"If Grace took Colleen away from us, Josh would be destroyed. He loved Colleen as if they were husband and wife. He is much kinder to her than he ever was to me. If Grace exposed what he knew even just within the medical fraternity, Josh would be destroyed. If he went to the police, I don't think anything would come of it because Colleen is a consenting adult. It has been normal for her for a long time. Colleen is his choice. She is his wife if you want to see it that way. Colleen is his rock... his reliable partner."

"Let me ask a few other questions. Why did you have Hansie's bike repaired?" Lazelle changed the subject.

"It was beat up and had a broken spoke on the front wheel."

"Where was the repair done?"

"At the shop where we bought all four bikes."

"Please give us the name of that place before your go. His bike was gone for two days he says. Wednesday and Thursday."

"I can't remember," she replied.

"So let us come back to Anton Delaney. Are you having an affair with him?"

Emmie Van der Merwe laughed out loud. "Haven't you worked that out yet? I thought you knew…Anton is my brother."

CHAPTER THIRTY-NINE

The interview with Anton Delaney was a few hours after his sister. There were no lawyers present. Anton was on his own. All this had come suddenly upon him.

Lazelle jumped straight in. "So, you are Emmie's brother?"

"Yes," he responded.

"Then you are Afrikaans. Your surname name is de Villiers. Why do you go by another name?"

"I changed my name a few years back because I wanted a more English name and did not want to be associated with Afrikaaners. I am proud to have lost the accent and sound as Australian as you do."

"Why?" asked Lazelle. "And how is it that the hospital does not have on the record that you are related to the Johannes Van der Merwe family?"

"I have not made it known at the hospital. In my final high school year in Cape Town, I scored highly in my matriculation. In fact, I was Dux of my school, with almost perfect marks in my final biology and chemistry examinations. I applied for and won a fully paid scholarship to study medicine at Melbourne University. My parents were delighted. They could never have afforded to help me complete university. They were sorry to see me go. Personally, I couldn't wait to leave that country and become Australian.

"I came here twelve years ago and completed my university and medical degree. I am near completion as a surgical registrar and have had no endorsement or help from Johannes Van der Merwe. He is pleased to have me on his team whenever I am rostered. I have earned my place as a surgeon in my own right."

"What sort of childhood did you have? Emmie must be ten years older than you."

"Eight actually. I am thirty now. We were brought up in a strict Afrikaans family. Modest folk… low income. Lots of 'bible bashing' and very religious."

"You must have been living at home when Emmie had the baby Colleen. You would have only been eleven years old?" asked Lazelle. "Colleen must know of you?"

"Emmie says Colleen remembers me living with them and then leaving home. I guess she was maybe six or seven then."

"Does she know you are here?"

"They always knew I was a doctor in Australia. But as I've said, I have not stayed close to the Van der Merwe family. I was happy to be unknown to the children and I did not want to be part of their family life. They are quite strange."

"Dysfunctional?" asked Lazelle.

"Yes. Horribly so."

"If we go back to the night of the surgery, your wisecrack about a girlfriend being hot and cold was something Johannes jumped upon and made a snide remark to Francis Grace?"

"Yes. Josh doesn't know my current girlfriend, so it was random on his part. He knew that I had been informed by my sister a little about their situation with Colleen. And he was furious with the intervention that seemed to be happening because of Grace's friendship with her."

"Who is your girlfriend?" asked Lazelle. "Do you live together?"

"She is Anna Bolton at present. I say that because we have only been together for about four months. And no, we do not live together. We each have our own places. At my age I find it hard to commit, so there have been many relationships. My wisecrack about 'hot and cold' was not about Anna but about my experience with women generally."

"What did you do after the surgery that night?"

"I left the theatre as soon as we had closed and went home."

"Who do you think murdered Dr Grace?" It was a pointed question and there were no lawyers to fuss over.

"I don't know." His answer was without conviction and indeed he looked decidedly uncomfortable.

"How did you get home that night?"

"I drove my car. I park at the hospital garage when on duty."

"Please give my colleague the make and model of your car and registration number. And thank you for your time."

After writing down the registration details, Delaney left the interview room. Lazelle said to Kellogg, "I don't think he's telling us the truth. And indeed, finding the truth in this case is starting to feel impossible."

CHAPTER FORTY

They found the bike shop where the Van der Merwe's had purchased the four cycles. It was in an eastern suburb quite some distance from their home. The owner, a sole proprietor, remembered the family well. After all, the sale of four bikes at once was something unusual. He easily recalled Emmie bringing him a 26-inch front wheel two weeks ago.

"What was the condition of the wheel when you received it?" asked Lazelle.

"It was missing a single spoke. She left it with me for a day and I replaced the spoke."

"When was this?" asked the detective.

The owner looked at his handwritten records. "She brought it in Thursday morning soon after I opened, and I fixed it, and she picked the wheel up that same afternoon." Kellogg photographed the page for the record then continued taking notes.

"Can you remember how the spoke was broken?" he asked.

The shop owner looked concerned. "That's the funny thing about this repair. It wasn't a broken spoke so much as a missing spoke. And quite unusually, the spoke had been cut at each end so a 25 centimetres length of a single spoke was the product."

"Can you recall the nature of the cuts?"

"Well, yes. To replace a spoke, you must take the tyre off the wheel and there are places where the spoke is fastened on the other side of the wheel rim. I had to take out the two residual parts from the wheel before I could put the new spoke in."

"Can you recall what those ends looked like?" asked Lazelle.

"I do because it was so unusual. The spoke appeared to have been cut by sharp wire cutters," observed the shop owner. "One end was squared, and the other was a sharp diagonal cut. I can give you a spoke the same size and cut it like I remember it if that would help."

"Thanks," said Kellogg.

They waited only a few moments. The shop owner returned with the 25 cm length of bicycle spoke. It was flat and narrow, very firm, much the same as a BBQ skewer. The diagonal cut was very sharp, and with the square end inserted into a handle of some sort this would become an effective weapon.

"Did you ask her why the spoke was cut?" asked Lazelle.

"Not directly. I know I asked her what happened."

"What did she say?"

"Something about the bike belonged to her 13-year-old son and what do you expect. Somebody did something stupid."

"Thanks for your help," said Lazelle. He felt satisfied that at last they were making progress.

CHAPTER FORTY-ONE

That evening at the Van der Merwe home, the four sat around the table over a delivered pizza dinner. Everyone had now been interviewed by the police. Their lawyers had given Johannes and Emmie and Colleen complete transcripts of the first interviews. Transcripts of the interviews today were not yet available.

"I've read what was said in the earlier police interviews with Colleen, your mother and myself. I don't see anything in them that would cause us any trouble," said the surgeon. "So, what happened today?"

There was complete silence.

"What happened?" he repeated emphatically.

Again, a reluctance to answer.

"They know a lot," said Hansie.

"Like what?" asked his father.

"They asked me about you and Colleen. They asked me about my bike. They asked me what I knew about Colleen speaking with Dr Grace."

"And what did you say?"

"I told them I didn't know anything about you and Colleen. I told them my bike went missing being serviced at the bike shop. I told them that Colleen said she respected Dr Grace. Not much else. Anyway, what has my bike got to do with it?"

"I'm not sure," said Emmie. "What else did you say Hansie?"

"I told them I wasn't happy with you as parents as well. I wish I was in a happier family like my friends."

"You shouldn't say such things," Emmie said.

"That is disrespectful Hansie," said his father. "You have no right to talk that way. Now the police think we are no good as a family."

"That's the truth though. We know. They know. Everyone should know that this family is crap." The boy walked out of the room leaving the three adults alone.

"Hansie, come back here," ordered his father. The boy did not.

"What have you told them, Colleen? You are the one who has brought us all this trouble."

Colleen was appalled. "How can you say that, Josh? What has happened is because of you. And, you mother, are a disgrace."

Both parents took a moment to evaluate this accusation.

"Okay," said Colleen. "The first thing you need to realise is that the police are learning nothing from us. They already know most everything. The questions being asked of us now are because of what other people have told them. We are only there to confirm or deny what they already know. We are not giving any new information…this family, the way we live… is all out in the open.

"They know Josh has been having sex with me since I was ten. That is an age when I could do nothing to defend myself. It is a bit late to ask… but Josh, why? You should have cared for me as a little girl and never let such a thing happen. And mother, how could you stand by and watch him do that to me?"

Emmie answered first. "I didn't know about it for a long time."

"You did. Nanna told you. You both lied to the police then and Josh you kept on doing it."

The surgeon became emotional and distressed. "It's not like that. I love you... look at us today. We are an adult man and woman. We are not related by blood. There's nothing wrong now."

"Maybe it is not criminal now, but it was back then," said Colleen. "I was too little to do anything to protect myself. What you have done to me as a child has scarred my life in future. You cannot ever pretend that grooming me into a way of life that has continued was not a crime. The police know Francis Grace was going to rescue me, and they have you and Mum as prime suspects for his murder."

"What nonsense," said the surgeon.

Again, silence.

"They are investigating the bikes and the missing spoke," said Emmie.

"What does that mean?" Colleen asked. "Why do you need to say that if it isn't going to somehow incriminate you? How could you put Hansie in that position if his bike was part of what has happened?"

"Let's all calm down," said the surgeon.

"I won't calm down," Colleen said. "I need to consider what Hansie, and I will do when you both go to gaol."

"Don't be so melodramatic," said Johannes.

Emmie said nothing. Another long silence... the three heads were bowed, not daring to look the others in the eye.

Johannes was the first to speak. "I know we will be further investigated, but it will go nowhere. We have nothing to hide. We are innocent. Our life will go on as normal. And Colleen, my dear girl, I will make it up to you. We will find a way to get back to normal. I have only ever loved you since you were a little girl. At first it was me being your stepdad reading you stories in bed. It was innocent. What happened afterwards, was loving. I never meant to hurt you."

And that was when Colleen walked out of the room.

CHAPTER FORTY-TWO

Lazelle and Kellogg went to the hospital security office and asked to see CCTV footage of the car parking building between 10 pm and 12 midnight on the Wednesday of the emergency surgery. They were particularly looking for the Delaney exit after the surgery. His car was quite a new BMW 320i sedan. They had his registration number.

They saw the car exit at 10:35 pm.

Expecting nothing more, the detectives were stunned to see the CCTV show Delaney return to the garage at 11:25 pm, his car with the back seats down and a view of some bicycle handlebars. The bike was laid out with the back seats folded down, from the boot through to the sedan interior. When Delaney got out of his car, parked in full view of the camera, he was still wearing his surgical scrubs.

Lazelle concluded Delaney had rushed from the theatre to meet someone on the outside who had the bike, and then brought it back to the hospital. Or, he might have fetched the bike from a place he left it, made the attack himself, and then put the bike in the car. They observed that by 11:40 pm he had changed into his street clothes and then driven from the hospital car park with the bike still in his car.

They knew from previous interviews that Johannes Van der Merwe had left from the front of the hospital and walked home. From the CCTV photos, he was seen and identified by his wife and family leaving about the time of the murder happening.

"Time to pick up Delaney and bring him in," said Lazelle. "If necessary, you can arrest him on suspicion of being involved in a conspiracy to murder."

Delaney was confronted mid-morning at the hospital by DCs Wells and Long. They had not formally placed him under arrest and conceded, so as not to make a fuss, that the man could walk out with them to the unmarked police car. There was no disturbance. No flashing lights. No uniformed police. No handcuffs. All very civilised. Delaney complied without any resistance or comment. They seized his phone and it was immediately given to Georgie to find out what communications happened on the days before and after the murder.

Not long later, he was seated in the interview room with Lazelle and Kellogg. They read him his rights. They told him he could have a lawyer. The surgical registrar was in a state of shock and remained quiet but shaken. He seemed very pale and dry in the mouth. They gave him a tumbler of water and he drank holding it with both hands that were shaking so badly that the water spilled. Not the steady hands of a surgeon. More those of a man now under immense pressure with something to hide.

"I don't want to comment without legal representation," said Delaney. Though shaken he was thinking clearly. "And it is important that it is not the same firm representing my sister and her family. I have a friend from university in a small firm here in the city. Can I call him please?" They were obliged to agree, found the number, and gave him an outside line to make the call. The lawyer came right away.

He was about the same age as his new client. Though they were studying in different faculties, they had met at university. His name was Brad Younger, and he was a junior partner in a firm with some criminal case experience. The first thing he requested was that he should be allowed time to speak with his client and find out what this was all about. Again, Lazelle had no option but to comply.

The interview began nearly three hours after Delaney had been brought to HQ. Lazelle took the lead. Kellogg sat in and made all the introductory statements and explanation of rights. He started the video recording.

Lazelle began. "Dr Delaney is here on suspicion that he is a conspirator in the murder of Dr Grace. We have CCTV vision of you Dr Delaney leaving the hospital garage in your car, after the emergency surgery," said Lazelle. "Then we see you return to the hospital still in your scrubs; your car's back seats are down and a bicycle is laid out from the boot into the interior of the car. You get out of the car to go inside the hospital and change clothes. Though it has not been made public, we have security footage of the murder being committed by a cyclist, stabbing Dr Grace with a bicycle spoke. What have you to say?"

The lawyer responded first. "Dr Delaney would like to make a statement." He turned to his client and said, "Go ahead."

Delaney read from a prepared statement.

"I did not know about or take part in the murder of Dr Grace. The analysis of my phone records will show there were calls from my sister the Monday before the day of the late surgery and the homicide. She asked if she could ride Hansie's bike to the hospital for me to put in my car on Wednesday. Then she wanted me to take it to a bicycle shop Thursday morning and leave it for service. The bike doesn't fit in her two-door sports coupe.

"At that stage we knew the surgical roster and I was on with Josh and the regular team from 11 am. We had a couple of scheduled operations and none of us knew we would be late with the emergency case. We all thought we would be ending our day late afternoon.

"Those arrangements were actual phone calls so you can check the numbers, but the real proof about what I am saying is backed up by subsequent texts. When we are working, we text and don't call. From memory, she was texting me about when I could bring the car to a nearby location about five minutes from work. That seemed absurd, and so I said I would meet her in the hospital car park and asked her to bring the bike there.

"There are texts that show me telling her of the late surgery and that we didn't know when it would end. She came back to say she needed me to let her know. Then as it got late, she said she was waiting nearby in Collingwood and as soon as I was done could I meet her? She wasn't there and I texted her to say I was waiting. She replied right away and apologised, telling me she was going to be a few minutes late. She didn't get there until after 11:15 pm and I was very annoyed with her standing me up for such a long time.

"You must understand most times I think my sister is mad, and you already know she does crazy things. Anyway, as soon as the surgery was over, I drove to her, waited, picked up the bike, and then went back to the hospital to change out of my scrubs and drive home.

"The next day she met me at the bicycle shop out east in Box Hill, and I went to work. And that's my story. She told me she was going to take the front wheel off and then the bike would fit in her car after the service. I wished she'd thought of that in the first place and not messed me around."

He put down his prepared notes.

"How was she dressed and how did she act when she met you to give you the bike?" asked Lazelle.

"She was in a full Lycra suit and helmet as she normally is when she rides her bike."

"Was she wearing a raincoat or dust coat?"

"No," Delaney replied. "Just the Lycra suit. She was going to walk home I guessed. She was agitated, very nervous and almost incoherent. When I asked her what had happened, she just told me to forget it and walked away. I was tired. I was annoyed. I didn't offer to drive her because I was still in scrubs and anyway, it is not far to her home. To me it was an absurd episode that I didn't understand at the time."

"Okay," said Lazelle, "but there must have come the time when you realised Dr Grace had been killed and that a cyclist had been responsible?"

"You know there was no mention of a cyclist or how he was killed for many days. All I knew was that he passed away on a train. I had no idea that a cyclist had stabbed him. I had no reason to think there was any connection between the murder, the bike and Emmie. Then my sister met with me over dinner one night recently and again the next evening at my house and she told me that she was in trouble."

"What exactly did she say?"

"She said that she had ridden her bike into Dr Grace that Wednesday night, and she had hurt him. I was appalled to be in the middle of it all and told her so. She had implicated me as an accessory to murder."

"Did she tell you she attacked Grace with a bicycle spoke?"

"Yes."

"Would she know enough to be able with a single blow to pierce the heart and be sure the victim would die?"

"No. And to be honest in a flurry of maybe colliding on a bike, no one could be sure of stabbing and causing death... I couldn't do it. And this is my concern, she wouldn't act alone. Josh is involved. As mad as she can be, I reckon he has something to do with it all. It is way too clever of him to be walking out the hospital in the front entrance and in plain sight to go home and her doing the deed of her own accord.

The family is nuts. I know it. You know it. That's why I really have always insisted on having my own life away from the lot of them."

"If what you say is true, you are still guilty of withholding information from this investigation. It seems to me you knew of your sister's involvement in this case and did not tell us when we interviewed you here just yesterday. That is a charge of perverting the course of justice, and it may be seen that you have colluded with those responsible for the murder."

The lawyer, Mr Younger asked for his client to be released as soon as the information from his phone had been verified. Lazelle informed them that Delaney would remain in the police cells for at least 24 hours while they arrested his sister and until charges had been filed.

Georgie brought the call records and transcripts of texts from the surgical registrar's phone. She went through them all with Lazelle and Kellogg. The numbers and texts substantiated all that Delaney had said. However, whether it was intentional or not, he had become an accessory to murder.

CHAPTER FORTY-THREE

DCs Dave Wells and Sam Long arrested Emmie Van der Merwe as she was lunching with some socialite friends in an upmarket South Yarra restaurant. This time it was formal. They announced that she was being arrested on the suspicion of the murder of Dr Grace. They read her rights out loud in front of the assembled diners. Handcuffs, police car with flashing lights on the kerb outside. The rich women who frequented this society landmark were 'gobsmacked' into silence. The detectives confiscated her phone.

A dozen mobile phones in the restaurant instantly made calls to husbands and partners at the top end of town, themselves with many personal contacts. Senior journalists in the media had the story within a few minutes.

Her lawyers were at police HQ within the hour and were allowed to consult with her. Lazelle informed Ms Wallace and Mr Wilson that they had evidence to show that Mrs Van der Merwe had stabbed Dr Grace that fateful night. He didn't say anything about her brother and the bike. He just left them on their own. No doubt the lawyers would be interrogating their client to find out what the police knew that she hadn't told them.

With both brother and sister in custody, Lazelle asked Superintendent Pizzey to make an urgent appointment with the police prosecutor in the presence of a senior lawyer in the State Attorney-General's office.

It was not long before Johannes Van der Merwe turned up at HQ. He asked to speak with his wife. Lazelle denied him access, saying she was under arrest and would not be allowed to speak with family. The surgeon asked after his brother-in-law, Anton Delaney. Lazelle said he was also being detained as a possible accessory. Van der Merwe could speak to neither.

They left it for more than three hours and it was already well into the afternoon when Lazelle and Kellogg interviewed Emmie Van der Merwe in the presence of her legal representatives. They outlined all that her brother had said and then asked her to explain.

"Mrs Van der Merwe does not wish to comment at this time," said Ms Wallace.

"Is that your position?" he asked Emmie.

"Yes. On the advice of my lawyers, I have no comment."

"You have been charged with murder. You will be remanded in custody until you appear in court," said Lazelle.

CHAPTER FORTY-FOUR

Pizzey, Lazelle, and Kellogg met with the Police prosecutor, Allie Bennett, and a senior State prosecutor Mr Lachlan Smart QC, in the Attorney-General's department to outline their case and findings. Such meetings took place to assess if they would be able to successfully win a criminal case if it went to court. And often, the meeting helped the police to focus on and gather whatever final evidence was required.

With all the known information on the table, the appropriately named prosecutor Smart QC, a very capable barrister, listened intently to Lazelle as he addressed the issues. This was the man who would lead the prosecution in the Supreme Court if the trial went ahead.

Lazelle spoke, not as he would to his team, but in clear, logical, and almost legal language. Pizzey was always impressed when his man took over like this. So was Ms Bennett... it made her work as Police prosecutor easier. The other homicide teams would mostly leave her to write the briefs from their formed opinions about the evidence. She did the grunt work at the end. Not so with Lazelle.

Kellogg also marvelled at these moments. He could not help but imagine that Lazelle, if arguing as a barrister in court, would have been something worth seeing. He seemed to know what was expected. And Lazelle knew, a conference such as this was an important moment to build some early enthusiasm to prosecute the case. He did not let such moments slip away.

"As to motive," Lazelle began, "there seems reasonable evidence that the girl was in a continuing close relationship with Dr Grace. She seems to admit he knew all about her having been groomed and sexually abused by her stepfather from the age of ten. He was appalled and wanted to help her. Because of what he knew, Grace despised Johannes Van der Merwe. Whether he was going to use what he knew formally, or just help the girl leave home, the Van der Merwe family structure and way of life was severely under threat.

"As to the actual crime, there seems reasonable evidence to support the allegation that Emmie Van der Merwe tampered with a spoke on her son's bike. I am almost sure that the missing spoke was the murder weapon, though I can think of more deadly ways to be sure to kill a man than this. But we are talking about a woman who was a paramedic with a husband and brother who are heart surgeons.

"I think the son's bike was chosen because it had all sorts of marks and scratches and the act of dropping the bike as an apparent accident at the crime scene would not be detected.

"We know she arranged for her brother to meet her soon after the murder, and that he loaded the bike in his car. When they met, she was dressed in Lycra and had her helmet, and except for the raincoat that she probably had disposed of, looked the same as the person in the CCTV footage we have of the actual assault. The brother says she was upset and almost incoherent. He went back to the hospital with the bike, changed, and went home. On the hospital garage CCTV, we can see the bike in the back of his car.

"The next morning, Thursday, he delivered the bike to his sister where she met him outside a repair shop. I believe she took off the front wheel and left it to have the spoke replaced. She must have driven the rest of the bike home in her smaller car. She collected the wheel that afternoon and must have put it back on the bike and it was in their home garage Thursday afternoon as normal. The son seems very sure the bike was missing on Wednesday, and he used it after school Thursday.

"The bike shop owner demonstrated the cuts on the spoke he had replaced. The diagonal cut one end and the square cut the other shows how one could produce a 25 centimetres long weapon. With a makeshift handle, the diagonal cut could easily have pierced a human body 20 centimetres through the heart if aimed correctly. In the shock of the attack there may not have been any substantial pain from the injury.

"On the matter of timing I think the murderer intended to do it exactly where it occurred, out of shot of the known hospital and public CCTV cameras. That would mean local knowledge and some research. Originally, she was planning an earlier assault, more like 6:00 pm. With the emergency surgery, that changed everything and put back the plan until late at night. And it was probably more convenient, and less likely to be seen, to do it all in the dark of night.

"As to who else is involved, I am inclined to believe the brother and his phone records prove what he said happened is true. I believe he knew before a recent interview that his sister was the assailant. He intended to withhold that information. The brother thinks Johannes Van der Merwe is also involved. The surgeon's alibi is to be seen on CCTV walking away out the front door of the hospital that night. He could not be the person who did the deed. With some further interrogation, his wife might incriminate him. There's no love lost between husband and wife. Delaney feels that she was coached as to how to stab Grace to cause probable death."

With that Lazelle concluded to allow Mr Smart to ask any questions or venture an opinion about the case. Smart took some time to consider what had been said, cupping his hands under his chin, elbows resting on the desk.

"Are the two youngsters involved?" he asked.

"I don't think so. The boy and his sister are close. Hansie's bike went missing as far as he knows. He needed to use it on Wednesday night and it wasn't there. He used it on Thursday after school to go to sports training. Colleen was very fond of Dr Grace. He offered her hope for the future, so she wouldn't hurt him and has been extremely upset about his death."

"Was the husband involved?" asked the police prosecutor. "Unless his wife tells us that, he cannot be charged."

Lazelle considered the question for a few moments. "We may get her to tell. It depends. She is the only one who knows. On the other hand, she may choose to leave him alone for the sake of her children."

Kellogg was quick to intervene. "She doesn't give a stuff about the children or her husband. It is all about herself and I think she'll cave."

Mr Smart continued. "And she refuses to be interviewed at present. Is that the case?"

"Yes," Lazelle replied. "The lawyers have silenced her."

"Well let's proceed with the hearing in the Melbourne Magistrates' Court to file charges. I'll schedule it for tomorrow afternoon, and I will need a concise brief in writing from you, Ms Bennett, to table with the Magistrate by 8.00 pm tonight. The defendants' lawyers will have to be advised of the time and place as soon as I know. Meanwhile, you can charge the woman with murder and her brother with perverting the course of justice."

The meeting ended and the policemen held their own briefing outside. Detective Superintendent Pizzey instructed Lazelle and Kellogg to assist Ms Bennett further so she could prepare the formal charges and written brief for Mr Smart. That was the process to be followed.

In preparing the file for the police prosecutor, Lazelle and Kellogg considered how the case might be defended by a sharp lawyer such as Ms Wallace, who was well-known as a very competent performer in court. Lazelle thought that this might end up a lesser charge, maybe manslaughter. No one can argue that stabbing someone with a bicycle spoke would undoubtedly kill. This may have been a warning for Dr Grace to leave the family alone. Did she say something to the victim? Did Grace know it was Colleen's mother? On the other hand, Emmie had planned the assault meticulously and the intent was certainly to stab Grace. If that caused death that is a murder charge under Victorian law.

The notes for the police prosecutor were prepared with all the known facts and emailed to her office by 7:00 pm.

Lazelle went straight home. He was pleasantly surprised to find that his daughter-in-law, Lily, who had a spare key for his apartment, had left a casserole in the fridge with a note on the kitchen bench, 'place in the oven at 180 degrees for 30 minutes.' He turned the oven on, put the casserole in, opened a bottle of Shiraz from the Heathcote regions, always good, and sipped his drink. After 35 minutes he refilled his glass and took the meal from the oven. It was wonderful. He phoned Lily and thanked her for her thoughtfulness.

Then he settled down with an after-dinner drink, Glenfiddich Scotch whisky with a smidgeon of water. Given all that had happened today he would sleep well.

CHAPTER FORTY-FIVE

They appeared in the Melbourne Magistrates' Court in the early afternoon for a preliminary hearing to file charges and confirm remand or set bail. The two cases were dealt with separately. In order of appearance, Anton Delaney came up first charged with perverting the course of justice in a murder investigation.

Delaney's lawyer friend Younger was assisted by a senior barrister that his firm had engaged. The defence argument was that Delaney had no knowledge of the crime but agreed that during a police interview he had misled the police about what he knew of his sister's activities.

The magistrate sent him to trial on the charge. Given the man was a surgical registrar with no criminal record and a career that helped save people's lives, bail was set at $50,000 on his own recognisance. He was free to go once bond was posted.

Emmie Van der Merwe was then presented to the court on a charge of murder. Lazelle observed that Johannes Van der Merwe, Colleen, and Hansie were all present.

Mr Smart QC, the prosecutor, outlined the case against the defendant using the Police prosecutor's (more accurately, Lazelle's) notes, and speaking most eloquently. Ms Wallace took her turn to appeal for the judge to grant bail. She said the charge was based on circumstantial evidence in that the defendant was not witnessed nor identified as the assailant. She appealed that the woman was from a good family and her husband, a reputable surgeon, would vouch for her. This was to no avail. The Magistrate, keen to do his duty and get on with a lengthy case list, confirmed that the defendant should stand trial for murder. She was remanded in custody until committal proceedings and then, ultimately, her trial in the Supreme Court of Victoria, which because of a backlog in cases, was likely to be scheduled four to six months hence.

The prisoner was allowed a moment with her family. It was tearful, even the surgeon wept. Hansie clung to his mother, Colleen cried. Emmie was handcuffed by prison officials and led away to the Melbourne Women's Remand centre.

Alone that night in her cell it suddenly dawned upon her that she would be in gaol for at least another four months no matter what she said or hoped would happen. This was the reality. This was happening. Her social life was history. The good life with everything paid for was a thing of the past. From now on it was prison clothes, prison food and only female company. The girl who never grew up was indeed now in Neverland.

That night Baz Kellogg received a phone call from his wife, Jennifer.

"How are you doing?" she asked.

"I'm okay, what about you?"

"It's been a hectic time finding an apartment and settling in. I will go into the office next week and that will be busy I am sure," she replied. "Are you doing well with your case?"

"We are not far off finalising things," he replied. There was a long silence before he added, "I miss you. This place is not a home without you."

"Let's leave it a while and then perhaps we can see one another again. I will have meetings at head office in Melbourne regularly."

"I'd like that," he said his voice beginning to quiver emotionally. "I've told Lazelle about our situation, and he is okay about me taking time off if you would like me to come to Perth."

"Not yet," she responded quickly. "Bye now," and she hung up abruptly.

He thought for a long time trying to recall every aspect of the very short conversation. It seemed to him that at least Jennifer had offered some hope that they might get back together again. He desperately wanted that to happen.

CHAPTER FORTY-SIX

Lazelle had slept well. The case that had preoccupied him for two weeks now was almost done. Two of the likely defendants were accounted for and would see their day in court.

He knew that the way forward with the case was to speak with Emmie Van der Merwe again, this time with the reality of her position staring her in the face. If there was more to tell they would hear it. He had emailed Sam Long to go visit her in the remand centre to just ask if she was okay and needed anything. Even though she was remanded only the day before, Sam made the arrangement for the visit right away.

They brought Emmie into a private interview room where she sat at a metal table opposite Sam. She was unshackled but a female warder remained in the room with them. Though Emmie knew Sam as a detective, the one who had arrested her, she had never been present at an interview with her.

"How are you doing?" asked the detective.

"Not well," the prisoner replied.

"I am here to tell you that if you have further information for us, we will help you all we can to moderate the charges and perhaps plead for a lighter sentence in court. As a member of the squad investigating this case, I know all the details and the one thing I am sure of is that you are not the sort of person to come up with an idea to murder someone. Everything I know about you is that you enjoy your life, you have friends, and you would not set out to destroy yourself. So, I just cannot understand what you have done and how it happened.

"Before you say anything I must warn you that what you say can be used in evidence in court. So, I am not asking you to further incriminate yourself. But I am asking you to explain how you came to this point?"

Emmie looked pensive. She was already aware that the case against her would look bad. Her lawyers, even the skilful Ms Wallace, had warned her that the evidence already presented was difficult to defend unless she started explaining why this happened.

"I am aware that I should have my lawyer with me now," she said. "I have waived that right to see you. Can I at any stage speak to you off the record?"

"No," Sam answered.

"Can you ask questions that I might not answer verbally but just nod my head?"

"No. However you respond I must note it. I am prepared to ask questions and you can answer me or not. For example, you seem to be the person least affected by anything Colleen had to say to Dr Grace. Your life was way out there in another place, almost divorced from the family. It seriously affected Colleen, and your husband because she was essentially his partner. It also affected Hansie because he was trying to look out for his sister. They were all emotionally involved, but you the least of all. So, I cannot understand your part in this. Why would you even contemplate trying to take Dr Grace out of the picture?"

"My future life, the way I wanted to live, would have been ruined if Josh was outed as a sexual predator and lost his job. If Colleen left home, he would have been devastated and I would have had to wear it. There are many reasons why the situation was going to change my life as well," Emmie replied.

"There seems to be no love between you and your husband, but he provides financial independence for you. You have apparently allowed your daughter from a young age to become his sexual partner. If you are found guilty of murder that's twenty years locked up. Your life is on the line, and I find it hard to believe that you did this alone. I cannot imagine you working on a bicycle spoke to make it into a weapon. Where did that idea come from?"

"I was a paramedic in South Africa. Josh was a cardiac surgeon. One of the random assaults in the streets, even in plain daylight amongst a crowd, would be for a thief to be first to bend over and help someone who had collapsed with a supposed heart attack. They had in fact stabbed the victim with a spoke. The thief they would look like 'a good Samaritan', shout "call an ambulance", rob the person and in the confusion that followed disappear leaving other people to help and comfort the victim. It was never meant to kill and rarely did. It was to simulate a heart attack for the perpetrator to steal a wallet.

"When we paramedics arrived on the scene, we would find the small puncture wound in the chest and we knew exactly what had happened. If it was serious, a heart surgeon, would patch them up. Josh had done that. The likelihood of a victim dying was low."

"Who made the weapon you used on Dr Grace?" Sam asked.

"I don't want to answer that at this time."

"If you did this and you knew Dr Grace wasn't going to die that's possibly a defence to murder and you might get off with a lesser charge. And let's suppose, he survived... how does any of this make sense?"

"Grace knew he was on dangerous ground. He knew Josh did not want him continuing his relationship with Colleen. Josh and Colleen did not want to be broken up."

"That's not what Colleen has told us, or what she is likely to say in court."

There was silence for some time.

"What will happen to my brother Anton?" Emmie asked.

"He'll get off lightly because all the phone messages confirm he didn't know what had happened until afterwards when you told him during your meetings. He is likely still to be found guilty of perverting the course of justice, because in a recent interview with us he did not tell the whole truth about what you had told him."

"Is that time in gaol for Anton?"

"Maybe, maybe not. He didn't know when you delivered the bike to him that night what you had done. Maybe he'll get a short sentence with the possibility of an early parole or even a suspended sentence. He has been forthcoming in telling us what he knows, and he will give evidence against you in court."

"What will happen to Hansie and Colleen?"

"I guess their life at home will go on with your husband. For what it's worth, I have spoken with Colleen, and she wants out and to have an independent life like any other young woman. I think she will want to marry, have kids and be a normal wife in a happy family. The situation she is in now is abnormal and has been created by your husband's perversion in grooming her from childhood. And because you let it happen. This will all come out at the trial because Colleen at least, maybe Hansie, will be called as witnesses."

Emmie seemed to become overwhelmed. She began to cry, and Sam handed her a tissue from a box nearby. The young detective did not feel sorry for her. She felt very sympathetic for Colleen. Sam was disgusted that Emmie had allowed her daughter to continue to be raped from the age of ten.

"I am not going to ask you anything more, Mrs Van der Merwe. You need to consider, even talk with your lawyers about how to mediate, and even soften the case against you. There are several options. The first is that the stabbing was meant to frighten Dr Grace and not kill him. The second is that it was not your idea. I'm guessing that your husband wanted Grace frightened as well and instigated the plan. Personally, I believe he made the weapon. If you became a witness to the whole truth, your sentence might be lighter.

"I don't know what your lawyers are saying, but the evidence has you at the scene, with a bike, dressed in Lycra looking like the person we see attack Dr Grace on a neighbour's security camera. You deliver the bike to your brother soon after the attack and you are at a bike shop replacing the spoke the next day. Your brother says you told him you were in trouble and you had run your bike into Dr Grace. You will not win this case and you will be found guilty. Help us and it could turn out much better for you."

After spending almost an hour to record her conversation with Emmie Van der Merwe, Sam reported back to Lazelle and Kellogg at HQ. The interesting new information was the South African experience that a spoke stabbing was meant to simulate a heart attack and facilitate a robbery. It seemed that the defendant did not mean to kill, and as premeditated as the attack was, the case could end up a manslaughter conviction.

Lazelle was puzzled. What was gained by an assault meant just to threaten? Though he might not be able to identify his attacker, Grace would have reported it to the police, and they would have gone through the same processes to know exactly what is known now. Even if Grace wanted to keep things quiet, he would have had medical treatment in St. Barts' emergency room, and the stabbing would have been routinely reported and become a police matter. It all would have ended up just the same as now, except Emmie would not be facing a murder charge.

From what Sam had told them of the interview at the remand centre, Emmie conceded she was the attacker but did not implicate her husband. Why not? Had they got it wrong?

CHAPTER FORTY-SEVEN

In his deepest thoughts, Lazelle was certain that the attack on Dr Grace was meant to kill. There was no other reason for it to happen unless there was certainty Grace would die.

He went back to the forensic laboratory. "Have you identified the stain on the inside right sleeve of the Lycra suit?" he asked.

"We cannot say more than it is a muscle relaxant," said the scientist. "It doesn't seem lethal in its current washed out state. Sorry... we need more time or more information."

He went to see the pathologist, Dr Kristin McClelland, who had attended the scene where the body was discovered and who had done the post-mortem the next day. They looked over the case notes and reviewed her findings.

"Here's my dilemma," said Lazelle. "How could any killer be sure that a stabbing with a thin bicycle spoke would end the victim's life? There is an unexplained stain on a Lycra suit that so far as we know is a muscle relaxant."

The pathologist referred to her file. "My notes are clear. Whatever was intended, the instrument penetrated the heart at a place where the person slowly bled to death internally. Poison did not come into it."

"Would you have found any traces of an agent in the body that might have been on the spoke that would guarantee death?"

"If you are talking about poisons, then toxins are able to be found if that is what you're looking for. Someone being slowly poisoned will almost always have traces in the system," she replied.

Lazelle thought for a moment. "The wife is charged with the murder, and she knew all about bicycle-spoke stabbings from South Africa, where she and her husband saw robberies happen while the victim was thought to be having a heart attack. I don't think she believed for a moment she would kill the man. She is a bit of a 'loose cannon' and probably doesn't think too clearly. Her intent was to scare Grace away from her daughter.

"I am also sure but can't prove it, that her husband put her up to this. And he would have wanted to make sure Grace died. He is a doctor; he is from South Africa. What might he have done to poison the weapon and ensure wherever she stabbed him in the heart he might have died for sure? And let's say it had been a poisonous weapon, would you have picked up traces of the poison?"

The pathologist looked a little concerned. "Given what I found at the time, that the victim died from internal bleeding caused by a stab wound, I had no reason to look further. There was no suggestion of a poison. And with the lapse of several hours, some acute poisons would have become untraceable anyway."

"Give me an example. Just hypothetical. I need to start somewhere."

Dr McClelland thought for a moment. "It's possibly an irony, but for example the victim, Dr Grace, would have been able to tell you all about the modern use in anaesthesia of what used to be tribal poisons used in South America and Africa. Why don't you talk to someone in that field?"

Lazelle phoned Kellogg and asked him to arrange a meeting with Dr Garry Johnson. They met at St. Barts hospital that afternoon. Dr Johnson was very wary, thinking that the detectives were going to take some sort of action because he had not been forthcoming sooner with vital information.

"Dr Johnson, we are here to ask your professional opinion as an anaesthetist, about the Francis Grace investigation. Mrs Van der Merwe has been charged with the murder and will stand trial. It appears she crashed into him on her bicycle near here and stabbed him with a bicycle spoke. Both she and her husband knew all about spoke stabbings because in South Africa they handled such cases. It was primarily done to have the victim fall, clutching his chest and the assailant would yell 'heart attack… get help' and then rob the victim and disappear in the confusion. It was rarely fatal. As a paramedic she might see the victim first, and he as a heart surgeon might have had to patch up serious cases in surgery.

"So, my dilemma is why would she stab him if she intended him to survive? And the alternative question then is, how do you ensure the victim dies? The pathologist tells me that the stabbing hit the 'bull's eye' in the heart, and he did bleed to death, even though that may not have been the intention. However, I want your thoughts about how with modern drugs, the spoke might have contained poison to make sure of the result."

Dr Johnson took no time to answer.

"Tribes in South America and in Africa used to dry a poison on the shaft of their arrows near the arrowhead. It was called curare and was a plant-based poison. It could be used on light arrows that would not kill immediately the large animals they hunted, but after an attack, they would stalk the animal for hours until it became eventually paralysed from the poison and died.

"In modern medicine curare is a drug belonging to the alkaloid family of organic compounds used primarily as muscle relaxants, being administered concomitantly with general anaesthesia for surgeries of the chest and abdomen. Dr Grace would have known all about this drug. It is an injectable form the way we used it. It could be reduced to crystals, crushed and melted into a paste.

"Dried on the shaft of an arrow it will dissolve quickly in blood. If it was on the pointed end of the shaft that pierced the heart where there is a surfeit of blood, it would cause the heart to slow, relax, it would cause low blood pressure and unconsciousness, and then paralyse the victim's breathing. Because the aim was true, the pathologist would not have seen any suspicious signs of asphyxiation."

"If we exhumed the body, could you find traces?" asked Lazelle.

"No. And even after the administration of the drug, traces of this toxin in a body wouldn't last more than eight hours. So, I'm not sure the pathologist would have found it during the post-mortem."

"Is there a register here at the hospital recording the dispensing of such drugs?"

"Of course. The protocols are very strict."

"Please can you take us the pharmacy and help us find out if this drug was dispensed in say, the two weeks before the murder? And who collected it?"

They went to the hospital pharmacy and looked through the register. There was only one transaction, so limited was the use of the drug. On the weekend before the murder, one ampoule of the drug Tubocurarine Chloride was signed out to Dr Grace. The pharmacist on the record was on duty then, so Lazelle, Kellogg and Dr Johnson were able to speak with him.

"Do you recall the transaction at all?" asked Kellogg.

"I do as a matter of fact. We are not allowed to give the drug to other than the qualified practitioner requesting it. The surgeon Van der Merwe came to collect the drug on behalf of Dr Grace. I had words with Mr Van der Merwe about that and he became irritated and insisted it was for surgery right away and that Grace was busy preparing the patient."

Johnson said to Lazelle quietly, "Francis would not have ordered this drug. It's not often used. These days there are many more modern ways to relax the muscles."

Lazelle asked the pharmacist, "If one was to distil this as a paste how could that be done?"

"Tubocurarine Chloride is prepared with a small quantity of the agent curare in a saline solution. If reduced, it would become crystalline. That might be crushed and if melted become a dark tar like sticky paste."

"Is there any way someone might be able to do that here in hospital?"

"Not likely. The smell would attract attention. If anyone was going to do that the ampoule would have to be taken away."

They checked the surgical log to see what surgeries were taking place on the day and at the time Van der Merwe collected the curare ampoule. That day Grace was not in the hospital and the surgeon was not rostered for any operation.

CHAPTER FORTY-EIGHT

Another warrant was issued to search the Van der Merwe home and the surgeon's consulting rooms and his hospital locker. The whole team took part. Reed and Wells took responsibility for the hospital rooms and surgeon's locker while Lazelle, Kellogg and Sam Long went to the house. Both Hansie and Colleen were there at the detective's request.

While the others searched, Lazelle sat with the youngsters in the lounge.

"I am very sorry about what is happening to your family. I know it must be difficult for you both. I imagine it is especially hard to have your friends know that your mother has been charged with the murder of Dr Grace."

They were both tearful but amazingly well composed. Lazelle was in awe of their maturity in such dire circumstances. Colleen answered first. "I knew something was wrong. Although my mother has always been remote, in the days after Francis's death she became too close to me, overcompensating and apologising for my sadness. Obviously if she did it, she knew how much it hurt me.

"Hansie and I talk to one another about what is happening. And you know what my plans were." She paused and looked squarely at Lazelle. "What are you looking for now? You have the bikes. You have my mother's things."

Lazelle didn't answer but rather asked a question. "Did either of you notice anything unusual the weekend or maybe a day or so before Dr Grace was attacked?"

They looked at one another as if there was nothing more to tell.

"Did you ever see your father, stepfather doing a science experiment in the garage?" he asked.

Hansie thought for a few moments.

"My Dad was doing something the Sunday afternoon before…" his voice trailed away. "I went to get my bike to go meet my friends and he was holding a small metal pan over a Bunsen burner. It smelt awful."

"What did it smell like?" asked Lazelle.

"Like roadworks. And in the confined space of the garage, it was very strong."

Colleen went back to her question. "What is happening now?"

"I can't tell you yet." He felt sorry for the young pair. "What I want you to do is to contact your grandparents in Cape Town and ask them to come here to be with you as soon as possible. If they want to talk with me, they have my number, and if we need to speed up visas for their visit, I will help you. And let me give you my personal phone number and if either of you want me to help in any way, call me. I mean it… I want to help you."

"Is something going to happen to Josh?" Colleen asked.

"You need your grandparents here with you. That's all I can say for now," the detective replied.

Lazelle sincerely hoped after all this was over, they might find a new life. Colleen would be free of her predator stepfather. She was old enough to be there for Hansie. The finances should work out okay once sorted. There were substantial assets the young ones could access. With the grandparents in Melbourne, they would surely have 'family' support and certainly get to know that Anton Delaney was their uncle. Hopefully, he might receive a suspended sentence and could be there for his niece and nephew.

Solving cases was one thing and that was his job, but the casualties always went far beyond the perpetrators. As he became older, Lazelle felt more and more sympathy for the suffering of the innocents left behind. In this case he had special feelings for the two youngsters.

The search revealed nothing. There was no evidence of the science experiment in the garage.

He telephoned forensics and briefed the scientist on their case. "You are looking for curare. Please analyse the stain for that. Do it as quickly as possible and let me know. It is urgent. Thanks."

CHAPTER FORTY-NINE

Colleen called Lazelle on his private phone number.
"You said I could talk to you. Can I speak with you personally?" she asked.
"Yes, of course," he replied.
They met in the Fitzroy gardens near the Van der Merwe East Melbourne home and sat together on a park bench in the shade of a tree. It was becoming a very warm day. Colleen looked like a frightened little girl. Lazelle was worried.
"What's happening?" he asked.
"I am afraid," she said. "Now my mother is in gaol, Josh is planning to take me away somewhere. He expects to get our relationship back to normal. I've told him I don't want to go anywhere with him. I don't know what to do. And he doesn't plan to include Hansie. I fear what he might do."
"That's not going to happen," said Lazelle thinking they would have proof enough to detain the surgeon within the next few hours. He couldn't believe the arrogance of the man who clearly thought he would not be found out for his role in the murder.

She continued. "You said you would help me and I would like you to understand me better."

"Go ahead. I promise this is between you and me. Colleen, I am on your side."

"From the age of ten, I have been groomed by Josh to become a sex partner. I didn't understand it. I was too young. I know now that it happened as he wanted it. In all that time I have not made any accusations.

"Since being in Australia and so far as this case is concerned, I am of lawful age in a consensual relationship. That is untrue... but it became a part of my life that I have had to accept to survive for many years.

"When you are a little girl and the new 'stepdad' in your life makes a fuss over you, buys you nice things, reads you bedtime stories, then cuddles you in bed it doesn't seem bad. It was a good feeling. But after a while he started to touch me and it hurt. I was quiet for a time but then told my grandmother, and she was rightly concerned. The police followed up and Josh threatened me that all the good things we had would be taken away from us if I said any more. My mother told me to not say such silly things and she didn't want to believe it at first. Though I now know she knew the truth and let it continue.

"As a teenager in South Africa I was not allowed to socialise with other boys. But there was one boy, I guess we were sixteen or so, and we got together after a school sports meeting on a late afternoon. I liked him. He tried to have sex with me, and I froze. I couldn't do anything... not because I didn't want to, the boy was very nice. I just felt dirty, and I didn't want him to be contaminated by what I had become. I don't think anyone who hasn't been through this can understand the intense feeling of being unclean... not normal... because of what has happened to you.

"My life since then has been to stay away from intimacy with any other man so they would never be spoiled by my past. I feel incredibly guilty, unworthy. I just don't feel I can ever have a proper loving relationship with a man... I want to... I want a husband and children... but the feelings I have from all that has happened to me are overwhelming.

"I guess you might ask how could I keep on having sex with Josh when I feel so bad? I have often kept him at a distance. I've tried to limit his activities with me, but he's the one who has had me since I was ten. I have been conditioned to accept and give in to his wishes. When it happens, I don't feel anything. Just numb... more of the same. There are things I can't get past... there are triggers he can use to have me. I know he really loves me. I justify he is not my father... not a blood relative. The act is not criminal now. But I know that what he has done to me was always wrong. And he has destroyed my innocence.

"That's the state of mind Francis Grace found me in, and he was a decent man. I told him what I have told you... not all at once but over a few meetings. Without pre-empting what you might be thinking right now, perhaps you might understand that Francis wanted to give me back my dignity. He wanted to help me get rid of the shame I felt as little girl and now as a woman. That is why he tried to help me... and that is why he was so disgusted with Josh."

She paused now, tears rolling down her cheeks. He reached out to her and put his arm around her shoulders. "You're not to blame. Colleen...you must tell yourself repeatedly, it is not your fault. You will get the chance to have a full and happy life."

Lazelle was moved... greatly moved. He felt so sorry for this young woman. More than that, he sincerely understood Dr Grace... now he knew how the man felt about Colleen. Now he, Lazelle, was compelled to do something. He knew he should pick up where Francis Grace left off. Her story made him feel the same. Lazelle needed to rescue this girl.

"Colleen. I understand everything you have told me. Your pain has developed over nearly ten years, and it will take some time to resolve. I will recommend some counselling with the police psychologist. You are entitled to this as a victim of a crime. Let me arrange that for you. And I want you to call me, talk to me any time. I am not Dr Grace, but I certainly know what he was thinking before he died. He was a good man. He's gone, but now I will help you."

They sat quietly for a time then the man took his arm away from her and stood up.

"Come with me now. I will walk with you to your home. Call your grandparents and I will fast-track them coming here. Do it right away. And you have my number. Call me anytime."

CHAPTER FIFTY

Forensics came back to Lazelle with a positive match. The faded stain on the inside sleeve was confirmed as a paste of the poison curare. It had no potency in the stain but could nevertheless be identified. Some of the paste that was on the end of the bike spoke had obviously been rubbed off on the inside sleeve of Emmie's Lycra suit where she concealed the weapon just before the attack.

With that information and the other evidence collected about Johannes Van der Merwe obtaining the injectable solution from the hospital pharmacy, having lied about surgery that was not happening, and Hansie's recollection about the smells in the garage, Lazelle applied for an arrest warrant. When he and Kellogg went to execute the warrant, the surgeon was not in his consulting rooms, nor at home.

Lazelle phoned Colleen and the call was not answered. He rang Hansie who was at school, and he didn't answer. Sam Long telephoned the principal's office and asked for Hansie to call urgently. When eventually his call came though Lazelle spoke.

"Hansie, it's Detective Inspector Lazelle. Do you know where your dad is?"

"He drove me to school and went on to take Colleen to university. We all left the house together," replied the boy.

"Colleen is not answering her phone," said Lazelle. "Neither is your dad at the hospital, in his rooms or anywhere to be found. Have you any idea where they might be? Is there a place you know about where they might go?"

"No. The only place I can think of is Phillip Island. Dad loves it there. He might have taken her on a picnic but really, I don't know. Call my dad's number."

Lazelle knew that it would be on file, but he was beginning to panic, "Hansie... tell me his number please."

Lazelle called Johannes Van der Merwe. The phone answered.

"It's Detective Inspector Lazelle. Mr Van der Merwe, where are you?"

"Why do you want to know?"

"We need to see you again urgently. And where is Colleen?"

"She is with me."

"Please let me talk to her."

"No. We are going away." Then the surgeon ended the call and hung up.

Lazelle alerted the Phillip Island police, giving them the licence plate number of the car and descriptions of the surgeon and stepdaughter. He asked them to speak with every hotel and motel on the island, and at San Remo just across the bridge on the mainland.

He also put out an all-points bulletin, searching for the surgeon who was now wanted for murder. Police throughout the state would be watching for the car and a man and a woman described in the urgent bulletin. All airports would be alerted. Flight departures out of Melbourne would be watched. International flights would be screened at passport control points. State borders were under observation.

Lazelle would never forgive himself if he couldn't get Colleen safely out of her stepfather's clutches.

CHAPTER FIFTY-ONE

Three hours later, the local police in Gippsland, southeast of Melbourne, reported that the Van der Merwe car had been seen by the ranger at the entrance of Wilson's Promontory National Park. The local police had within thirty minutes closed the sole entry point and were present in the little village and camping ground at Tidal River. The car was found, and its occupants gone. Wilson's Promontory was so large, with so much bush, mountains, beaches, gullies, and rugged terrain that finding the pair might not be easy.

Lazelle and Kellogg were flown by police helicopter to the area where their priority was to hover over visible grounds near Tidal River. In a relatively short time, they spotted two figures at the top of Mount Oberon, a rocky outcrop of grey granite boulders with lichen painting the rocks in patches of vivid orange. The two figures were on a cliff edge that from hundreds of feet above overlooked the beach and the village. It was not an official lookout. There were no guardrails there. With binoculars, Lazelle easily identified the couple as the surgeon and Colleen. "That's them," he said and handed Kellogg the binoculars for his confirmation. Lazelle feared something terrible might happen to Colleen.

Lazelle rang Van der Merwe again. He answered. "Is that you in the helicopter?"

"Yes," responded the detective. "It's time for you to stop this. I know you love Colleen, and you don't want her to suffer any more... she needs to be set free Josh," he said using the man's familiar name for the first time.

"If we can't be together, I will throw us both over the edge." Lazelle heard Colleen scream in the background, "Josh no... please no."

"You really don't want to do that to her Josh."

"I will... just back off."

"Okay but please stay put. We will land on the beach, and I will come up to you and we can talk. You are an intelligent man, and you know that right now you're upset. That's not the frame of mind to make any rash decisions. Will you agree to wait for me to come see you?" asked Lazelle. "I'll come alone."

"Okay," the surgeon said. "I will talk with you but no tricks."

They landed on the beach. Kellogg stayed at Tidal River and would liaise with his boss by phone. Lazelle had two uniformed officers drive him in a police car to the parking area of Mount Oberon where he climbed the last very steep 400 metres. The two police officers, a man, and a woman, climbed with him and stayed out of sight only 50 metres away. Lazelle climbed to the summit and stayed 15 metres short of Van der Merwe and Colleen.

They were very close to the edge of the cliff. Colleen was bound by plastic cable ties with her hands behind her back. She was defenceless and trembling with fear.

"You understand that I will take us both over the edge here if you make the wrong move," said the surgeon.

"Okay," said Lazelle. "I am going to stay here." With that he removed his jacket and placed it on a rock nearby. He sat on his jacket. He was badly out of breath. The day was sunny and getting very warm.

"So, what do you want?" asked Van der Merwe.

"I want to help you."

"You want to arrest me for murder. I'm pretty sure you know enough to do that. And I can see all the police there." He indicated towards the police cars he could see down at Tidal River.

Lazelle was quiet, gathering his breath and thinking. Then he said, "The park is closed, and police have the place cordoned off. I would like you to talk to me about Colleen. I know you love her deeply. She knows that too. But you cannot want to kill the beautiful young woman you love. It doesn't make sense. She has so much to look forward to and surely you must want her to have a happy life in future. I know you want that."

That seemed to agitate the surgeon and he looked confused and unable to be consoled.

"Josh, you have been a doctor for a long time and a great surgeon. You have spent many years looking after the health of people. With your surgical skills, you have saved many lives. The people you have saved you never knew and now, because of you, they are free to enjoy the rest of their lives. It would be against everything you stand for, all your training, all your work, all your values as a person, to destroy a life... especially the life of someone you love. You must allow Colleen to walk away from this. There is no alternative."

Lazelle remained quiet and observed the surgeon taking his hands away from Colleen who edged a little further away from the cliff edge without his intervention. Van der Merwe was folding and unfolding his hands. Then he instinctively ran one hand through his hair and clasped the other around his mouth. He was a broken man and looked capable of doing something irrational.

"Josh... please let Colleen walk to me. I will assure you that she gets all the help she needs in future. That is my sincere promise to you."

He continued to clasp his hands to his head and face, clearly experiencing great emotional pain. He said nothing. He made no move to keep Colleen from walking slowly to the detective. When she reached him, Lazelle took her arm firmly and whispered, "Go down the hill a little further and there are two police ready to look after you. Don't look back and don't say anything to me. Keep walking."

She walked slowly down the track and disappeared out of sight.

Lazelle continued to keep eye contact with the surgeon. "Thanks Josh. You have just proved your love for Colleen."

The surgeon asked, "What is going to happen to me?"

"We'll go back to Melbourne together. I promise you will be comfortable and afforded every courtesy. We have evidence that suggests we can arrest you for the murder of Francis Grace but that has yet to be tested in court. There will be a trial. You will have good legal representation. The process will be fair to you.

"I can remember my wife often saying to me 'one day at a time' during the difficult years of my life. I think you should be prepared to take it one day at a time," Lazelle concluded.

"I'll go to gaol. It will be a long sentence. I am not sure I can do the time."

"Again, we haven't reached that point and even if that happens someone like you will be a tremendous help to others and an important person. Just step back from the cliff, maybe sit on the rock there, I'll sit here. We can be quiet. Take all time you want."

"How can you help Colleen?"

"For a start, I have fast-tracked visas for her grandparents to come here and be with Colleen and Hansie. I will arrange for Colleen to have a police psychologist counsel her... that is usual for those people affected by a criminal proceeding. Hansie and Colleen have my mobile phone number and they can call me anytime. As you and Emmie face the legal proceedings, they will both remain at home, with family, and I give you my word, I will personally watch over them."

The surgeon slumped onto a nearby large rock and turned his head to look out over the beach, the rolling surf, and rugged mountains nearby. The sky was clear of any clouds and a perfect deep blue. Lazelle, in other circumstances, felt he would think it was the most beautiful view that he had ever seen, and he had never been to the promontory before. However, he could feel his heart racing because of the perilous nature of this situation. He needed to concentrate and not be distracted.

They sat there in absolute silence for a few minutes, but then two TV helicopters arrived and started filming from 500 feet above. Monitoring police radios was normal practice and transmissions about this situation had happened from almost the first sighting of the couple. And so, the story broke. Lazelle was furious. He picked up his phone and while Van der Merwe could hear him, he telephoned Kellogg, ordering him to contact the media to get the helicopters the hell out of there. After two or three more minutes they disappeared and silence resumed. He felt the silence was working to his benefit in trying to have the surgeon give himself up.

They sat in complete silence for another twenty-five minutes. It was hot. Very hot. Lazelle felt unwell.

Eventually, Lazelle said quietly "Josh, let's go get a drink. I'm hot and thirsty. How about you?"

Without saying anything more, Johannes Van der Merwe walked to Lazelle, who simply took his arm, no cuffs, no aggression, just a hand on his arm as they walked back to the police car where Colleen and the two police officers were waiting. She sat in the front, a policeman and Lazelle sat either side of the surgeon in the back, as the policewoman drove the ten minutes to Tidal River.

Journalists and TV reporters were all over Lazelle as he emerged from the police car. Kellogg made sure Van der Merwe was taken inside to a private room and away from the fuss.

"I have no comment. Please give us some space," is all the detective would say.

After some time for a rest and refreshment, Lazelle and Kellogg, with Van der Merwe in custody, flew back to Melbourne.

CHAPTER FIFTY-TWO

Van der Merwe's lawyers were quickly on the scene at Homicide HQ. Ms Wallace and Mr Williams were both in attendance as Kellogg made the formal charge of Johannes Van der Merwe. With all the formalities out of the way, the surgeon declined to answer any questions on the advice of his lawyers.

Lazelle asked for a private conversation with the legal pair.

"I am going to give you a 'heads up' about what we know. It will be disclosed to you anyway as we prepare for the trials. I think it is difficult for your firm to properly represent both Emmie and Johannes Van der Merwe unless something changes.

"She did the stabbing and has all but confessed. She didn't think he would die and so that might be possibly viewed as manslaughter if she cooperates.

"However, the husband made sure Grace would die, by falsely obtaining a dispensed anaesthetic derived from curare, a poison used by tribes in Africa on arrows and spears to kill large animals. He distilled the phial of the hospital medicine to crystals then melted them to a dark sticky paste. I suspect he made the weapon, then dried the paste on the sharp end for a few centimetres down the shaft. Emmie had no idea that he had put poison on the spoke. We have enough evidence to prove he did this, and his premeditation and clear intent was that Grace would not survive. This is murder. And we can also charge him with kidnapping and threatening to kill his stepdaughter.

"I am suggesting that you decide which party to represent or, if you decide to do your best for both clients, then Emmie Van der Merwe might tell us all she knows and become a witness for the prosecution at the trial of her husband. Or he could plead guilty and be looked upon a little more leniently. It's up to you."

Ms Wallace, who would be the leading barrister for the defence in court, thought hard about what Lazelle had said. At this stage they did not know how much the police had by way of evidence.

"I appreciate your candour, Detective Inspector Lazelle. Let us talk with both the defendants and get back to you. This might take some time."

That evening Lazelle went back to see the Van der Merwe youngsters with Sam Long. They were of course terribly upset and not sure what to do. He ordered some takeaway food and the four sat down together to talk.

"Your father has been arrested and both he and your mother will be charged with the murder of Dr Grace. He might also be charged with kidnapping you, Colleen. You both will be called as witnesses, so I cannot tell you any of the details, but I want to make sure you are okay. Have you reached out to your grandparents yet?"

"Yes, this afternoon. I just called them," said Colleen. "They are deeply shocked by what has happened and are doing their best to get here urgently. They must visit the Australian consulate to obtain visas."

"I have contacted the Australian Embassy in South Africa and have emailed details of this case. I have arranged for the consulate staff there to expedite the visas for your grandparents on compassionate grounds. The visas will be ready tomorrow and your grandparents can be here the day after."

"Thank you," said Colleen. Though she was clearly shaken by the ordeal she had just been through, Lazelle marvelled at her composure now. She sat with her arm around her brother. She was concentrating on supporting Hansie.

"Why are you doing this for us?" asked the boy. "Is it because you feel guilty for taking our parents away from us?" Hansie had tears in his eyes and the question was asked respectfully, not in anger.

"I've been a policeman for a very long time. I have seen many cases of people causing others to be hurt or killed. I guess you might say I have spent my working life thinking way too much about the dark side. I am deeply sorry about what is happening to you both. I think I can understand the pain in your hearts. I know you both deserve better than this. You have missed out on what most youngsters would call a normal happy family life.

"Right now, despite everything you have already been through, this is still going to be a most difficult time. Your parents are both waiting to be tried in court and will probably end up spending a long time in gaol. You must make your own way in life now. I want your grandparents to be here to help that happen and to support you. The days in court will cause you more pain, that I am afraid cannot be avoided unless your parents plead guilty.

"In speaking with you both throughout this case I have nothing but admiration for your intelligence and common sense. I know the future will come right for you. You can stay in your home, be together and have the support of your real friends. You don't know them so well yet, but your friends will be there for you. You did nothing wrong.

None of this is your fault. Please remind yourselves repeatedly… this is not your fault."

Colleen and Hansie were quiet. They both had tears in their eyes but remained composed. The boy looked at his hands.

"Did they use my bike to do this?" Hansie asked suddenly.

"I can't say more about what happened. If you are to give evidence, I would rather you say just what you know. Tell the truth when you answer the questions."

"When will the court cases be?"

"Not for some time unfortunately. About four to six months. So, you must get on with your lives… go to school, go to university. Your grandparents will be here so this can become a family home. And as I have said before… I will be your friend."

Throughout all this Sam Long had remained quiet. She said, "I guess you know Colleen how much has happened today and how hard it has been, not only for you, but also for Detective Lazelle. He must go home and rest now. I have brought my toothbrush and will stay with you tonight so that you are not alone."

"Thank you. I need you here Detective," said Colleen.

"Call me Sam."

Lazelle left the youngsters with Sam and went home. He felt overwhelmingly sad for them. He was tired of the hurt. He felt ill. Exhausted.

After he was gone Colleen said to Sam, "Why is he such a good man?"

Sam also had tears in her eyes. She had never seen her boss like this before. She wondered if any of their team really knew him. All she could say was, "He is a 'special man'. And he doesn't know how special he is."

CHAPTER FIFTY-THREE

During the night he woke with a crushing chest pain. He could hardly breathe. His phone was on the charger in the kitchen, and he stood trying to get to it. After a few steps he staggered and fell to the floor. The pain was enormous. He knew it was a heart attack. Unable to stand, he crawled five metres to the kitchen and pulled on the cord of the charger to bring the phone to ground.

They answered his 000 call. "What's your emergency?" the voice asked.

"Ambulance. Heart attack," he gasped. "Unit 4, 55 Honeypot Lane…" and he fell silent.

"What suburb?" the voice asked. But there was no answer.

He woke up in the Box Hill Hospital emergency room attended by a doctor and two nurses who were monitoring his vital signs. The pain was still with him. With the help of the phone company, they had tracked his location and the ambulance, with police attending, broke into his unit to find him unconscious on the kitchen floor. His heart was failing, and fortunately the paramedics were able to stabilise him.

"Where am I?" he asked.

"You are in hospital," explained the young doctor. "About an hour ago you had a heart attack, and it is good that we have you here so soon. A cardiologist is preparing right now to do an angiogram and see what needs to happen. You are in good hands."

They wheeled him away for the procedure. After it was over and he was back in a bed assigned to a ward, the cardiologist came to see him.

"It's good news Mr Lazelle. You had a blocked coronary artery that we have been able to stent. Because we have treated you very quickly the heart muscle is not at all damaged. So, after a rest, you will be good as new. We'll keep you here for a day or so and just monitor your recovery. Any questions?"

"Why didn't I have any signs before now?" he asked.

"You probably did but they would have been slight. Heavy in the chest, maybe real tiredness, out of breath going up stairs… that sort of thing. I'll leave you now to be with your son."

Andrew had been at his side since he had come out of theatre. "That's good news Dad," he said. "You will be okay now. We were worried. I came as quickly as I could. When I got here, they had you in theatre."

Lazelle closed his eyes for a few moments and said nothing. Then he looked at his son, eyes welling with tears. "I'm okay. Thank you. I think I would like to rest now."

"I'm not surprised Dad… after yesterday and now this, you must be tired."

He gently gave his father a hug and bade farewell. Having seen what his father had gone through on the television news last night, and now a heart attack, Andrew was emotionally upset and frankly appalled. There was nothing sensible he could think to say. Hero or not, his father should not have gone through that terrible experience.

THE INTROSPECTIVE DETECTIVE

The next day Baz Kellogg and Sam Long visited him. She brought some flowers, and he came with some chocolate. Lazelle appreciated their concern, though he didn't think the chocolate would go down well with the cardiologist.

"How are you doing?" asked Sam.

"I'm good. Apparently, they cleared a blocked coronary artery within an hour and a half of the event, and the heart itself isn't damaged. If I hadn't reached my phone and the ambulance didn't come, I would be dead."

"You're a lucky man," said Baz.

"What's happening with the case?"

Kellogg answered. "The surgeon has been remanded and will be committed for trial. We are waiting for an answer from the lawyers about whether to consider a plea from Emmie Van der Merwe. Otherwise, all is quiet."

Sam added, "You have no reason to rush back. The job is done. When you are discharged from hospital go home and rest. We want you fully recovered, fit and well when you return."

A nurse brought in some flowers and a 'Get Well Soon' card. He opened it and read the handwritten words.

> *Dear Detective Lazelle,*
> *We are thinking of you. Please get better soon,*
> *Love from us both.*
> *Colleen and Hansie. xxx*

He handed the card to Baz and Sam. They read it and when they looked back at Lazelle, he was crying, tears flowing freely down both cheeks.

Sam went to his side, sat by him, and held his hand. He seemed comforted by her. She said, "Both Colleen and Hansie are doing okay.

I will go back and be with them tonight and their grandparents arrive tomorrow. Now. Let's get you back to good health."

After a while he composed himself. "How can those kids care about me after what I have done to them?"

"You have not done this to them Sir," said Kellogg. "Their parents have done this."

Sam squeezed his hand. "You did your job. In fact, I know you have done so much more than anyone else could do. The Van der Merwe youngsters think you are a very special man. And so do I."

After a few days he was back home. Andrew and Lily wanted him to come stay with them, but he said he felt fine, and it would be quieter and more peaceful for him to be in his own place. And he did feel good. With a healthy heart there was a spring in his step. He was breathing more easily. He was more positive about the future.

Lily had brought food over so he could just heat up meals. She had done the grocery shopping for bread and milk. He was well supplied and had no reason to fuss about anything. After school, she brought the boys to see him. They spent two hours together. Both Johnny and Keith were on their best behaviour and sensitive to what Poppa had been through.

"We saw you on the TV Poppa," said Keith. "They said you caught a bad man and saved a girl from being thrown off a cliff."

"You're a hero, they said on TV," said Johnny. "My mates at school have been talking about you. My teachers have all told me I should be very proud of you."

"It's not really like that," said Lazelle. "Television makes things look exciting. They exaggerate. All I did was talk to a man who was very upset. And after a while he did the right thing."

"You're a hero... Poppa's a hero," chanted both boys over and over while stomping their feet and clapping their hands. They were so excited. He had to laugh.

"Don't be silly," he said. "I'm just your Poppa."

Lily smiled. "That's enough boys."

Though it was lovely to be with his grandsons, they wore him out. All the chatter. When they played about the house it was loud. He loved Andrew, Lily, and the boys so much. He was very thankful to have them in his life. They were even more important to him now after such a health scare. But he was relieved when they left.

Home alone it was blissfully quiet.

Andrew came by after work. "Dad, we have to talk some common sense," he said.

"Okay," his father said warily.

"You are nearly sixty-four years old and just had a heart attack. Your adventure at Wilson's Promontory is all over the news. You have had a torrid time. It must have been a lot of stress. It seems to me that your heart attack was brought on by the events of the day. Brought on by your work."

"Perhaps, but it was going to happen sometime because I had a blocked coronary artery, and all is well now. I am in good shape," Lazelle responded.

"Dad. I want you to think about your future please. You are comfortable in your home here. The police pension and your savings are enough for you to live well without working. After what has happened you can take sick leave and then access your pension and retire."

Andrew wasn't finished. "I have been a policeman's son, a detective's son all my life. I have had anxious moments worrying about you, but nothing like this. That was frightening. Not just for you but for me. I want you to be here for me and Lily and the boys for a long time. I want you to find a balance... no more drama. I don't want to lose you any time soon Dad."

He knew his son was talking sense. "You're not going to lose me. What happened has found out the heart condition and I was lucky. Now it will be watched closely. I'll have medicines. All will be well," he promised. "But I hear what you say... I'll seriously think about it."

Andrew cut a baguette into slices, and they shared some of the minestrone Lily had made. They ate heartily, dipping bread chunks into the soup. They laughed about the boys chanting "Poppa's a hero" and stomping about the house. When they were finished Andrew gave his dad a hug and went home.

Though he was probably not meant to, Lazelle poured himself a single malt Scotch that evening and sat comfortably in his favourite chair. It was sobering to be in a quiet zone recovering from a near-death experience. Strangely he felt differently about some things. He had survived, and the question now was, what would he do with this second chance?

He thought about the Van der Merwe youngsters. They were such lovely young people. He wondered how they had achieved that given the selfishness of the parents. He thought about the difficult times they were about to go through. Intellectually he knew he had done the right thing as an investigator. But emotionally he was finding it very difficult to cope with their forgiveness. How could they send him a card, how could they write 'love' to him when he was the reason, they had lost their parents?

THE INTROSPECTIVE DETECTIVE

He tried to understand Colleen who from a little girl had been groomed and sexually abused and who had no real relationship with her mother. And Hansie, a boy fast becoming a young man. Both well-educated, but now they were going to need the strength to survive the embarrassment brought upon them, to ignore the journalists and the media, to be involved with the court cases and somehow come out the other side intact.

Would they let him help them in future? He hoped so, for he wanted to be there for them.

CHAPTER FIFTY-FOUR

Baz Kellogg called his wife Jennifer in Perth. It had been a week since she first called him.

"Hello Baz," she answered seeing his identification on the screen.

"Hi Jen… how are you?"

"I'm fine. Busy though now that I'm into full swing in the office."

"Where are you staying?"

"I've rented a flat in Subiaco. It was empty so I moved in straight away. It's just a short drive to the city centre."

Baz paused and waited for her to say more. He didn't want to be sounding like a detective. Then she spoke. "What is happening with your case Baz?"

"It's over so far as I am concerned. We've arrested the surgeon and his wife, and they are remanded in custody. There will be all the usual court appearances, that will happen in time. But our investigation is done. The only thing left is to give evidence in the trials."

"That's good."

"There has been a casualty though. Lazelle had a heart attack and was in hospital. But they stented a blocked artery, and he is okay now."

"Oh." Jennifer for a moment was speechless. "It's a tough job being a homicide detective and you know I have always worried about that in our relationship."

"I know. That's why I am calling. I guess this case and you leaving me has given me many reasons to consider my future."

She waited for the rest of his thoughts.

"I am willing to resign here and perhaps join the WA Police in a desk job, sort of regular hours work, if you will give me another chance Jen. I've made some enquiries, and it looks like it could happen quite easily."

She was quiet for what seemed an eternity. "Can I think about it Baz, please?"

"Of course," he replied.

"I'm coming to Melbourne to Head Office Tuesday next week and would be happy to have dinner with you, in a restaurant, not at home. Would you be willing to do that? We can talk some more."

He felt elated. "That would be wonderful. Text me when and where and I'll be there."

"Okay… see you then," and she rang off just as he said, "I love you."

A week later they met for dinner precisely at 6:30 pm on the Tuesday. Baz made sure he was not late and that the job could not be blamed for interrupting their possible reconciliation. The restaurant was in Lygon Street, Carlton… a famous Italian area with many pizza places and better class ristorantes. She had chosen a place that they had been to before and they sat inside with a view of the street and the alfresco dining area.

She was there first and as he approached the table she rose and kissed him lightly on the lips. He kept one hand by his side and with the other touched her lightly on the arm.

"How did your day at Head Office go?" he asked.

"All good. They are pleased with what I am doing in Perth. What's news in your case?"

"Mr Johannes Van der Merwe has been charged of murder. He, and his wife are both remanded in custody until their committal hearings probably in four months' time. After that there will be separate trials in the Supreme Court, rather than the one trial where both husband and wife would be in court together. It's all with the lawyers now."

"Sounds like it is all over for you now. How are you?" she asked.

"I miss you. I love you. It has been difficult for me to be alone and not have you with me at home." He wondered whether that was an appropriate thing to say given they had just met, and he wanted dinner to go smoothly.

"I know," she said but added no more.

The waiter came by with menus. They ordered their food; she wanted gnocchi and he asked for spaghetti Bolognese. They both ordered an Aperol Spritz.

"Have you thought some more about me coming to Perth Jen?" he asked her.

"Yes. But not yet. I need to get to a place where my day is routine. Now I am in a new city which I really like, with a new job, living in a new apartment, and I want to make it all my own. I want to feel comfortable."

"Do you have a social life?" he asked wondering if there was another man.

"Not yet. But I can go out with some of the colleagues in the office for dinner now and then."

"Is there another man, even just a friend?"

"Yes. My deputy is a single man in his forties and has been out to dinner with me just the one-time last week."

"Do you have any feelings for him?"

"I like him very much," she had a wry smile on her face. He was confused, it was like she was teasing him.

"What do you mean?"

"He's a gay man… a very nice companion. Baz, I'm not interested in any other man at this time. In fact, I am probably trying to take a rest from having a partner and the last thing I want right now is to enter another romantic relationship."

They smiled happily together for the first time in a long time it seemed.

"Do you still love me?" he asked while they were in this jovial mood.

"I have only ever loved you and there has never been anyone else. These past two years our love has cooled off. I am unable to feel emotionally attached to you right now. As I said, this is a rest for me. I don't know if I still love you… we will have to work on that if we want a future together." She stopped talking and took both his hands in hers across the table.

"Are you willing to try and work on it with me if I come to Perth?" he asked.

"As I said, let me get settled and into a routine that feels normal. I'll tell you after that happens."

They parted with a more serious hug and a kiss. He felt they had made progress and she promised they would speak every week. She would call first then he the week following. Keeping in touch that way they felt things might become clearer.

CHAPTER FIFTY-FIVE

A few weeks later, a conference was convened in the Attorney-General's Department between Ms Wallace SC, Mr Williams from Patterson & Partners, Mr Lachlan Smart QC the Crown prosecutor, the Police prosecutor Ms Bennett, Superintendent Pizzey, DI Lazelle, and DS Kellogg from the Homicide squad.

Ms Wallace had asked for the meeting and so was invited to take the lead by Smart.

"We are aware of most of the evidence gathered now against our clients. The briefs seem to sum things up well. Of course, what our clients have told us is privileged information, but we believe that Mrs Van der Merwe had no knowledge of the poison, and she wants to make some sort of arrangement with the State to give evidence that will tell all she knows if the charges against her can be reduced to manslaughter, and she pleads guilty." Wallace stopped and waited for Smart to respond.

He took his time and apparently habitually, adopted the pose Lazelle had witnessed before, cupping his hands to his chin and resting his elbows on the table while he considered his reply.

"I have reservations Ms Wallace. However, you want to explain it, Mrs Van der Merwe planned and prepared to attack and stab the victim who eventually died from his wound and not because of the poison. What do you think DI Lazelle?"

"You are right. Almost accidentally she stabbed him in exactly the right spot to kill. It has been referred to me by the pathologist that she hit the 'bull's eye'. The poison was not needed. But all the evidence shows, and the pair of the defendants knew, such attacks rarely killed anyone in South Africa. To put it mildly, she was silly to do it in the first place in the hope that Dr Grace might leave her daughter alone.

"We have enough evidence to make the case that the husband knew what she was doing, and by adding the poison to the bicycle spoke he certainly intended that the weapon would kill Dr Grace. We don't know for sure whether Dr Grace would have died from the poison had Mrs Van der Merwe not struck the 'sweet spot', but it certainly seems highly likely. I agree with Ms Wallace the wife had no idea about the poison. It's your call Mr Smart."

"What do you feel should happen Superintendent Pizzey?"

"They both must be judged and do gaol time. A violent crime was committed causing death. Whether Mrs Van der Merwe believed death was inevitable or not, she is the perpetrator of what was a planned assault resulting in death."

Smart turned to Kellogg for his opinion.

"Like DI Lazelle, I have been at the centre of this case for a month or more and it has been disturbing for us all. It is not just about murder but also child sexual abuse and negligence in parenting. The Van der Merwe's have treated their children horribly. Hiding behind a professional career and lots of money they have already got away with 'murder' colloquially speaking, long before the death of Dr Grace. I have no sympathy for either of them. I know this is not about anything else than the murder case. Personally, I am sorry they will not be tried together so the whole truth could come out."

Smart thought for a while longer. Then he asked, "If she tells all, what are we going to learn that we don't already know? What evidence can she give in her husband's trial that will help us anymore?"

"She can fill in the details," said Lazelle. "A lot of what you have is circumstantial where her husband is concerned. We concede she can be identified as the assailant so to plead guilty saves a trial in what is now a huge backlog of cases. She can tell us when the idea to attack Grace was formed. What did they both really know about Colleen and Grace? Did they make the plan together? Why didn't she know about the poison? What did the husband do after Grace's death? What were the conversations at home? What ways did they think they could deny the charges and get away with the crime? Where did the murder weapon end up? What did she do with the raincoat? You all know that with her evidence on the record the trial against her husband is a 'slam dunk'."

Smart then made his decision. "Very well, if she pleads guilty and makes a statement now and will give evidence at his trial, we can reduce the charge to manslaughter. The court can then look leniently on her, and we can agree a sentence of say ten years rather than twenty. With good behaviour she might be out in seven years.

"May I ask," asked Smart, "how is your firm able to represent them both?"

Williams answered. "We can't if we proceed this way today. Clearly our interests now are to represent the woman. However, we can ask another Senior Counsel to take on the defence of Johannes Van der Merwe, give him all we know, and he can choose to be instructed by another firm of solicitors. We would tell the client we have a conflict of interest, given the evidence that she did not know he had poisoned the bicycle spoke."

Two days later, Emmie Van der Merwe was in the interview room with the prosecutor, her two legal representatives, Lazelle, and Kellogg. The interview was being video recorded and would certainly be used in evidence. With the formalities addressed and the identification of all present, Lachlan Smart QC asked the questions.

"Mrs Van der Merwe, you have been charged with the manslaughter of Dr Francis Grace. In view of the various discussions with your lawyers and they with me, are you prepared to plead guilty in the case against you and to testify in the murder trial of your husband Johannes Van der Merwe?"

"Yes," she replied. "I will plead guilty to manslaughter."

"And in return, we the prosecution are prepared to look leniently upon your case and plead to the judge for a lighter sentence. You must understand the judge will have the final say. But he or she will take your co-operation into consideration."

"Thank you."

"When did you and your husband plan this attack? What were you thinking at the time?"

"It started around six or seven months ago when my husband found Colleen crying on Dr Grace's shoulder the night he came to our home for a pizza between hospital meetings. In the weeks that followed, Colleen seemed to be becoming more and more interested in someone else. Josh guessed it was Grace. Her relationship with my husband was getting frosty. I don't know how he found out, but somcone told him they had seen Grace and Colleen having lunch seated together on a park bench not far from our home.

"He confronted Colleen, and they had a blazing row. She admitted that she was in touch with Francis Grace, but they just talked. There was nothing more to it, she said. Grace was a friend not a potential partner.

"She also added that she had every right as a nineteen-year-old young woman to plan to be with a proper husband... with her own home, and her own children. She quite plainly told him that this was her childhood family and like every child growing up she wanted to leave here and find her own way in life.

"I suppose about a month before the incident, my husband and I discussed what would happen if Colleen left home. Was Grace helping her? Was she going to be with him? We didn't always believe it was a non-sexual affair, after all, she was intimate with her stepfather, and he was around the same age. We didn't know if she had told him about our family. We didn't know if a prude like Grace would report our weird situation. You know the downside, I am sure. Our way of life, as bizarre as it might seem, was satisfactory for Josh and me and we didn't want it to change. He told me he was trying to intimidate Grace at work, but that the 'cold English bastard' gave nothing away.

"Colleen said nothing more, but it seemed she was planning to leave home. She was giving away clothes to the charity bins. She was organising herself to move out into her own place. Josh became obsessed with the damage now evident in his intimate relationship with her and told me Grace had to be warned off."

"What is the timeline and what happened?" asked Smart.

"About a week before, Josh came up with the plan as you know it. Use Hansie's bike, I was the best rider, and he would fashion a bicycle spoke to do a stabbing like we had seen done in South Africa. It wouldn't kill him but frighten him off. On the Sunday before the attack, I have been told by my lawyers that Josh made the poison. I wasn't home. Apparently Hansie remembered a bad smell. I swear I had no knowledge of that.

"I knew he cut the single spoke from Hansie's bike on the Wednesday morning and then I hid the bike meaning to ride it to hit Grace after surgery late afternoon or very early evening. I repeat, I did not know that he had poisoned the spoke. He must have pasted it that morning. He gave it to me and showed me how to place it in my sleeve ready to do the stabbing. We didn't need to say much about where to stab because as a paramedic I was always listening to the heart beating in patients.

"That Wednesday was all over the place with the late emergency operation. My brother unwittingly became involved at my request to pick up the bike from me after the act and deliver it next day to meet me at the bike shop."

Mr Smart folded his arms and leant on his desk. "Did your children know anything about this?"

"No, never."

"You seem cold-blooded about what you did. You talk about knowing where to stab the victim. Doesn't that mean you knew how to kill? If that was not your intention, how was this going to warn him to stay away from Colleen?"

"No. It means that where I thought to stab him would cause a pain in his chest and he would seek help. The hospital was right there. As to how it would keep him away from Colleen I really didn't know. Obviously, Josh knew because of the poison that it would end the man's life. But I didn't know. It all seems ridiculous now."

"Did you say anything to Dr Grace after the collision? Do you think he recognised you?" asked the prosecutor.

"We did speak afterwards; it was just an apology as if it was all an accident. I said sorry and he just said it's an accident. No harm done. He was decent. Not at all the stuffy Englishman that I had been led to believe."

"Do you think he recognised your Afrikaans accent?"

"No. I said a few muffled words and I tried to sound different."

"Was there any stage when you were afraid? Did you want to pull out and not go ahead with this?"

"Yes. Often, I had the overwhelming urge to give it away. But the pressure from Josh was unbearable."

"Then tell us about the actual assault."

"I rode at him and at the last second it looked like I had lost balance and would fall. I was totally in control and for me I did the bike crash routinely; the actual deed was done cleanly and with great calmness. It was almost like being back on the street as a paramedic and I had to do this to save the patient. Stupid way to think, I know. And after I had done it and when I delivered the bike to Anton, I was a complete mess."

"You walked home and obviously your husband was there. Where were Colleen and Hansie?"

"The kids were in their rooms and asleep at that hour. This is around midnight. Josh was home and waiting to hear from me. I told him that I had done it all very smoothly. We talked about what might happen next. I said Grace would survive and go to the police. They would investigate his situation and it would lead to us. We had better be able to tell a convincing story.

"Then he told me Grace would be found dead on the train. Even then he didn't mention the poison. He seemed to convince me that the way I did it would end the problems we had. He acknowledged the police would be speaking with us because we were part of Grace's professional life and dependent upon what Colleen might say we could be seen to have a personal interest in the man."

Lachlan Smart leaned back in his chair. "Thank you for your candour. One last thing, where did the weapon and the raincoat end up?"

"The weapon had a handle that was made of duct tape and two wooden slats. It was narrow enough to be concealed along my arm and up the sleeve of my Lycra body suit. I disposed of it in a recycle garbage bin between the attack site and where I met my brother. I threw the raincoat into a charity bin quite near the hospital."

The meeting ended with the prisoner being taken away. The lawyers left. Only the police and prosecutor remained.

CHAPTER FIFTY-SIX

Lazelle asked Mr Lachlan Smart QC if he might make a further representation.

"Go ahead.," said Mr Smart.

"It's about Dr Anton Delaney and the charge of perverting the course of justice," he said. "To my mind he knew nothing about the attack during the time he was helping his sister by collecting and delivering the bike for her. The first he knew of perhaps her involvement was when she told him days after the murder. He did not know a bike was involved until she told him. Nobody did, because we kept that information hidden from any publicity.

"In the first interview with us he told the truth. He did not know otherwise; we did not know to ask, and he didn't mention the collection of the bike from his sister. In our second interview he did not say what his sister had told him about her involvement. That is the core of the charge against him.

"With both the mother and father going to gaol, their youngsters, Colleen and Hansie will have their grandparents from South Africa here for a while, but it would also be very helpful for them to know their uncle. He could become an important new stabilising influence in their lives. He is a surgeon. His work is lifesaving. He is a good man caught in a situation not of his own making.

"So, I ask whether the charge against Delaney might be mitigated in some way? In my experience this is not at the high end of perverting justice."

Smart cupped his hands to his chin. That was clearly his thinking pose.

Kellogg spoke before any answer. "I can only agree with DI Lazelle. The bike was a hidden issue when I first spoke with the man. He couldn't have suspected anything, and we didn't know what questions to ask."

"What do you think Superintendent?" Smart asked Pizzey.

"I have no objection. I take it Delaney will give evidence if required?"

"I'm sure he will Sir," added Kellogg.

Smart took a while longer deliberating. "Okay. I will withdraw the charge and advise the court that the prosecution does not wish to proceed with the case."

"Thank you," said Lazelle.

At home Lazelle settled into his evening meal routine. He drank a Scotch whisky while he heated a prepared meal from the store. He had long run out of Lily's meals and had to resort to grocery shopping. Not being a particularly keen cook, he preferred microwaveable meals.

In all respects, the Grace murder investigation had been a difficult case with many twists and turns, and he and his team had worked professionally following the clues that led to this result. Now he must consider his own position. Where was he about continuing work? What did he feel were his other options? Never mind all the advice, this was his life and he needed to decide what would make him happy.

And that was the word that had always haunted him... a state of mind that constantly eluded him... happiness.

Yet after his heart attack, he felt obliged to take advantage of his second chance at life. He knew that he might easily have died if they had not found him. He felt well now and able to do anything he chose. There was a new optimism, a chance to be diffcrent. And that did not necessarily mean giving up his job. He liked his work, but it had to be a part of his life, not the sum of it. Balance was the answer. He could help the Van der Merwe kids, but they would move on. He had Andrew, Lily, and the boys... that was a constant.

He needed something more.

CHAPTER FIFTY-SEVEN

Jennifer called Baz at home.

"Hello Baz. How are you?"

"Hi Jen. I'm fine. What about you?"

"I'm calling to tell you something," she said.

His heart began pounding in his chest as he waited for her news. Quite quickly she spoke. "I feel settled here and yet something is missing." She waited for him to say something.

"What is that?" he asked.

"You. Please come and be with me."

There was a long silence, and she couldn't quite make out what was happening. Baz had started to quietly sob and found it difficult to speak.

"Of course, I will," he managed to say.

"Are you crying?"

"Of course, I am."

CHAPTER FIFTY-EIGHT

That evening the team met to celebrate the closure of the case. There would be evidence some of them had to give at the trial. There would be things to do to provide answers for the prosecution to help with their presentation of the evidence. Otherwise, their work was done.

Detective Superintendent Pizzey called them together in the Homicide HQ meeting room. He was obviously elated that such a high profile and difficult case had been solved.

The media had sensationalised the Wilson's Promontory arrest. They were reporting the released details; Lazelle's spectacular rescue of Colleen and his ability to talk the surgeon down from a possible suicide. He was to be recommended to the Governor for a high bravery award.

All the detectives were widely commended. There was no doubt Pizzey had been under personal pressure from his superiors including the Chief Commissioner and the State Police Minister. The 'Super' was relieved and enthusiastically thanked the team. He congratulated Lazelle for his concise management of the investigation. They were glad it was over. Baz Kellogg seemed exceptionally pleased about something and could hardly wipe the smile from his face.

They all decided to go for a drink after work to celebrate. Lazelle joined them for a very short time, just the one beer, then excused himself.

He went to East Melbourne to the Van der Merwe home. He was warmly greeted by Colleen who gave him a hug and Hansie who clasped his hand in a vigorous handshake. They appreciated the several times that he had been to see them or telephoned to make sure they were coping well. By now he knew and liked their grandparents, Mr and Mrs de Villiers, who had arrived from South Africa two days after the rescue of Colleen. They were good people.

Anton Delaney was there as well, reunited with his mother and father and Colleen who remembered him from when they lived together, she a child and he a teenager. She loved being back with him. Though Hansie had never known him before, he was very happy to have an Uncle Anton… a younger, reliable man in his life. Anton was fun for a teenage nephew.

Though Lazelle had said nothing, Anton Delaney knew from his lawyer that his case was dropped because of the senior detective's representations.

Lazelle admired the family unit that they had become. And he was delighted and proud to have been able to help create a new happiness for the youngsters, Colleen and Hansie, who were facing up bravely to the coming trial. This was why he loved his job so much and why he would keep doing it as long as he could.

CHAPTER FIFTY-NINE

Lazelle called at the Victorian Deaf Institute to tell Anne Grace personally that the investigation was over. He had previously cleared her insurance claim as she and Grimaldi were no longer part of the investigation.

The receptionist paged Mrs Grace and she was surprised to see the detective in the foyer. "Could I have a word Mrs Grace?" he asked. "Certainly," she said and led him to a small meeting room nearby.

"You already know I am sure, but I wanted to tell you myself, that the Van der Merwe husband and wife have been charged with your husband's murder. It is all over. You can get on with your own life now."

"Thank you," she said. "It has been difficult."

"How are you doing?" he asked with compassion.

"Much better. The girls are more settled. My parents have been a big help and I have my routine. It is sad to say but given the way Francis worked, and with his long absences from home, it is not so different now. But we miss him. There's not the familiar face around anymore."

"I'm glad you're okay. I'm sure it will get easier in time." said Lazelle.

There was a silence and she waited for him to take his leave. He didn't.

Instead, he signed, "Can I join your class here for a little while? I want to see what you do."

She signed "come with me" and they went to a classroom with just eight children of various primary school ages. Signing to the children she introduced him as a policeman. "You can ask him anything," she said. Lazelle was quite taken aback to be thrown into the 'deep end'.

So, the signing session began.

"Do you catch bad guys?" one little guy asked.

"Yes. But you know it is not always about bad guys. I help the good guys too." He became emotional thinking about the sufferings of Colleen, Hansie, Anne Grace and even his own narrow escape from the heart attack that nearly killed him.

He spent an hour with the class, silent except for their laughter and murmurs of approval. He told them how as a little boy he had a deaf sister. He told them that his Mum, Dad, and he and his sister Cathy, signed all the time in the house. They never wanted to leave Cathy out of a conversation. He said they never spoke, and their house was silent. He told them he was happy signing with them now because he really liked the quiet. He would rather sign than talk. He didn't like loud voices and noises.

When he stood up to go, the children signed to Mrs Grace, "He's a nice man." And they all applauded him as a thank you for spending some time with them. Lazelle felt deeply moved. He was a little confused... he had discovered something about himself.

Anne Grace saw him out. In the foyer she said to him. "You're a natural. Will you join me here from time to time in future? Become a volunteer. What do you think?"

He didn't hesitate. "Yes," he said. "I want to do this. For the kids of course... but for me as well. Today I felt a freedom that has long been missing. I have found it easier to sign than to speak. Perhaps that's a message... something I need to acknowledge. Signing was all about respecting my sister Cathy. To speak and engage socially with others has been hard. I am often uncomfortable in social situations. It is my work habit... not my preference.

"So, I would love to help you. And being here will help me... probably as much as we might help the children. Thank you sincerely Mrs Grace."

"Call me Anne" she said.

"And I'm Robin."

Late afternoon there was a knock at the front door. It was Andrew. His father settled comfortably in his favourite chair with a Scotch in hand. Andrew pushed aside his mother's array of cushions and sat on the couch with a small bottle of mineral water.

"I'm just on my way home from work and thought I'd come by to see how you are Dad. You look so well... and happy. The case is done. What else is happening?"

"I've just spent today at the Victorian Deaf Institute with Anne Grace. I had a wonderful session with children, signing and answering their questions. I enjoyed it so much that I have joined them as a volunteer. I am going to help at least one day a week."

Andrew was speechless. He looked flabbergasted.

"Part of me has been missing," Lazelle laughed softly. "Today, I was signing again. I was part of something positive and innocent. I was honouring my sister Cathy and I felt she was with me today. This is a perfect complement to my work and I can't wait to go back again next week."

"I am so happy for you," Andrew's voice choked up with emotion. He was so proud. "The boys are right, Dad. You really are a hero."

Milton Keynes UK
Ingram Content Group UK Ltd.
UKHW050622311024
2487UKWH00068B/841